Benjamin Leopold Farjeon

Aaron the Jew

A Novel: Vol. I

Benjamin Leopold Farjeon

Aaron the Jew
A Novel: Vol. I

ISBN/EAN: 9783337044756

Printed in Europe, USA, Canada, Australia, Japan

Cover: Foto ©Andreas Hilbeck / pixelio.de

More available books at **www.hansebooks.com**

AARON THE JEW

VOL. I

AARON THE JEW

A Novel

By

B. L. FARJEON

AUTHOR OF

"*Great Porter Square,*" "*Grif,*" "*Blade o' Grass,*"
"*The Last Tenant,*" *etc., etc.*

IN THREE VOLUMES

VOL. I

London, 1894

HUTCHINSON & CO

34, *PATERNOSTER ROW*

CONTENTS OF VOL. I.

BOOK THE FIRST.

MOTHER AND CHILD.

CHAPTER V.

BOOK THE SECOND.

RACHEL.

CHAPTER X.

CONTENTS.

AARON THE JEW.

—◆—

BOOK THE FIRST.

MOTHER AND CHILD.

CHAPTER I.

THE POOR DOCTOR.

ON a bright, snowy night in December, 1871, Dr.
Spenlove, having been employed all the afternoon
and evening in paying farewell visits to his patients,
walked briskly towards his home through the
narrowest and most squalid thoroughfares in Portsmouth. The animation of his movements may be
set down to the severity of the weather, and not
to any inward cheerfulness of spirits, for as he passed
familiar landmarks, he looked at them with a certain
regret, which men devoid of sentiment would have
pronounced an indication of a weak nature. In this
opinion, however, they would have been wrong, for

Dr. Spenlove's intended departure early the following
morning from a field which had strong claims upon
his sympathies was dictated by a law of inexorable
necessity. He was a practitioner of considerable
skill, and he had conscientiously striven to achieve
a reputation in some measure commensurate with
his abilities. From a worldly point of view his
efforts had been attended with mortifying failure ;
he had not only been unsuccessful in earning a bare
livelihood, but he had completely exhausted the
limited resources with which he had started upon his
career ; he had, moreover, endured severe privation,
and an opening presenting itself in the wider field
of London, he had accepted it with gladness and
reluctance. With gladness, because he was an am-
bitious man, and had desires apart from his profession ; with reluctance, because it pained him to
bid farewell to patients in whom he took a genuine
interest, and whom he would have liked to continue
to befriend. He had, indeed, assisted many of them
to the full extent of his power, and in some instances
had gone beyond this limit, depriving himself of the
necessaries of life to supply them with medicines
and nourishing food, and robbing his nights of rest
to minister to their woes. He bore about him dis-

tinguishing marks of the beautiful self-sacrifice. On
this last night of his residence among them, his
purse was empty, and inclement as was the weather,
he wore, on his road home, but one thin coat,
which was but a feeble protection from the freezing
air, which pierced to his skin, though every button
was put to its proper use. A hacking cough, which
caused him to pause occasionally, denoted that he
was running a dangerous risk in being so insufficiently
clad ; but he seemed to make light of it, and smiled
when the paroxysm was over. In no profession can
be found displayed a more noble humanity and
philanthropy than in that which Dr. Spenlove
practised, and, needy as he was, and narrow as had
been his means from the start, his young career
already afforded a striking example of sweet and
unselfish attributes. In the Divine placing of human
hosts, the poor doctor and the poor priest shall be
found marching in the van side by side.

During the whole of the day snow had been falling,
and during the whole of the day Dr. Spenlove had
had but one meal. He did not complain ; he had
been accustomed to live from hand to mouth, and
well knew what it was to go to bed hungry ; and
there was before him the prospect of brighter times.

But cheering as was this prospect, his walk home through the falling snow was saddened by the scenes he had witnessed in the course of the day ; and one especially dwelt in his mind.

"Poor creature!" he mused. "What will become of her and her baby? O pitiless world! Does it not contain a single human being who will hold out a helping hand?"

Before one of the poorest houses in one of the poorest streets he paused, and, admitting himself with a private latchkey, unlocked a door on the ground floor, and entered a room which faced the street. There was a wire blind to the window, on which was inscribed,—

CONSULTATIONS FROM 9 TILL 11 A.M.

This room, with a communicating bedroom at the back, comprised his professional and private residence.

Dr. Spenlove groped in the dark for the matches, and, lighting a candle, applied a match to a fire laid with scrupulous economy in the matter of coals. As he was thus employed, his landlady knocked at the door and entered.

"Is it you, Mrs. Radcliffe?" he asked, not turning his head.

"Yes, sir. Let me do that, please."

The paper he had lit in the grate was smouldering away without kindling the wood ; the landlady knelt down, and with a skilful touch the flame leapt up. Dr. Spenlove, unbuttoning his thin coat, spread out his hands to the warmth.

"Any callers, Mrs. Radcliffe?"

"A gentleman, sir, who seemed very anxious to see you. He did not leave his name or card, but said he would call again this evening."

"Did he mention the hour?"

"Nine, sir."

Dr. Spenlove put his hand to his waistcoat pocket, and quickly withdrew it, with a smile of humour and self-pity. The landlady noticed the action, and dolefully shook her head.

"Very anxious to see me, you say, Mrs. Radcliffe."

"Very anxious indeed, sir. Dear, dear, you're wet through!"

"It is a bitter night," he said, coughing.

"You may well say that, sir. Bad weather for you to be out, with that nasty cough of yours."

"There are many people worse off than I am, without either fire or food."

"We all have our trials, sir. It's a hard world."

" Indeed, indeed!" he said, thinking of the female patient whom he had last visited.

" Where's your overcoat, sir? I'll take it down to the kitchen ; it'll dry sooner there." She looked around in vain for it.

" Never mind my overcoat, Mrs. Radcliffe."

" But you had it on when you went out, sir? "

" Did I ? Don't trouble about it. It will dry quickly enough where it is."

He was now busily employed making a parcel of books and instruments, which he had taken from different parts of the room, and which were the only articles of value belonging to himself it contained. The landlady stood for a moment or two watching his movements, and then she hurried down to her kitchen, and presently returned with a cup of hot tea. As she passed through the passage, with the cup in one hand and a candle in the other, she glanced at the empty umbrella stand.

" His umbrella, too, as well as his overcoat," she muttered. " The man's heart's too big for his body ! "

She re-entered the room.

" I've brought you a cup of tea, sir, if you don't mind taking it."

" Not at all, Mrs. Radcliffe. It is very kind of you."

He drank the tea, which warmed him through and
through.

"We're all sorry at your leaving us, sir," said the
landlady. "There's plenty that'll miss you."

"I am sorry, too," he replied; "but when needs
must, you know. I can do no good to myself or
others by remaining. If the gentleman calls again,
ask him to wait, if his business is of importance.
You had better tell him I am leaving Portsmouth
to-morrow morning."

With his parcel under his arm he left the house,
and trudging through the snow again, halted at a
pawnbroker's shop, lingering awhile before he entered,
as sensitive men do before putting the finishing touch
to a humiliating act. Then, shrugging his shoulders,
and muttering, "I ought to be used to it by this
time," he plunged into the shop, where he obtained
upon his few last treasures as much as would pay his
third-class fare to London and the two weeks' rent
he owed his landlady. Thus safe-guarded for a few
hours at least, he left the shop, but instead of immediately retracing his steps to his lodgings he
lingered once more irresolutely, with the air of a man
who was at war with himself upon a momentous
question. The sixteen shillings due to his landlady

was in his pocket, and undoubtedly it was but simple honesty that it should be handed over to her without hesitation. But the hapless female patient who had occupied his thoughts during the last hour was at this moment in the throes of a desperate human crisis, and dark as was the present to her suffering soul, the terrors which the future held in store for her were still more agonising. She had a young baby at her breast ; she had no food in her cupboard, not a loaf of bread, not a cup of milk ; she had not a friend in the world to whom she could appeal for help. She, too, was in debt to her landlord, a hard man who was waiting for another sun to rise to thrust her and her infant into the white and pitiless streets. It would have been done to-day but for the intervention of Dr. Spenlove, who had pawned his overcoat and umbrella to buy of the poor creature's landlord a respite of twenty-four hours. The sixteen shillings due to Mrs. Radcliffe would buy her another respite for a longer term, but when this was expired there was still the hopeless future to face. Dr. Spenlove thrust aside this latter con- sideration, and thought only of the ineffable relief it was in his power to bring to a heart racked with anguish and despair. He lost sight of the fact that the wretched woman would still be without food, and that she was too weak to work for it. Even when she was strong, and able to ply her needle throughout the whole of the day and the greater part of the night, her earnings had never exceeded six shillings a week; she had confessed as much to the good doctor, but for whose timely aid the work-house would have been her only refuge. As he stood debating with himself the sentiment of pity was strong within him, but he could not banish the voice of justice which whispered that the money was not his to dispose of. All the people with whom he was acquainted were poor, and his landlady was as poor as the rest; he knew that she often depended upon the payment of his rent to pay her own. It might be that just now she could afford to wait awhile for what was due to her; if so, he would dispose of the sixteen shillings as his benevolent instincts impelled him to do; he must, however, ascertain how the land lay before he acted. It may appear strange to many fortunate persons that issues so grave and vital should hang upon a sum of money which to them would not be worth a thought; but it would be a good lesson for them to learn that opportunities are not scarce for bringing Heaven's brightest sunshine to overcharged hearts by the judicious bestowal of a few small coins out of the wealth which yields them all the material comforts of life.

Having made up his mind upon the important matter, Dr. Spenlove turned homewards, and as he walked he recalled the incidents in connection with the unhappy woman in which he had played a part. She was a stranger in the neighbourhood, and had lived her lonely life in a garret for five months. No person with whom she came in contact knew anything of her or of her antecedents, and it was by chance that he became acquainted with her. Attending to his poor patients in the street in which she resided, he passed her one afternoon, and was attracted as much by her modest and ladylike appearance as by the evidence of extreme weakness, which could hardly escape the observation of a man so kindly-hearted as himself. He perceived at once that she was of a superior class to those among whom she moved, and he was impressed by a peculiar expression on her face when his eyes rested on her. It was the expression of a hunted woman, of one who was in hiding and dreaded being recognised. He made inquiries about her, but no one could give him any information concerning her, and in the press of onerous cares and duties she passed out of his mind. Some weeks later he met her again, and his first impressions were renewed and strengthened ; and pity stirred his heart as he observed from her garments that she was on the downward path of poverty. It was clear that she was frightened by his observance of her, for she hurried quickly on ; but physical weakness frustrated her desire to avoid him ; she staggered and would have fallen had he not ran forward and caught her. Weak as she was she struggled to release herself; he kept firm hold of her, however, animated by compassion and fortified by honest intention.

"You have nothing to fear from me," he said. " Allow me to assist you. I am Dr. Spenlove."

It was the first time he had addressed her, but his name was familiar to her as that of a gentleman to whom the whole neighbourhood was under a debt of gratitude for numberless acts of goodness. She glanced timidly at his face, and a vague hope stirred her heart ; she knew that the time was approaching when she would need such a friend. But the hope did not live long ; it was crushed by a sudden fear.

" Do you know me, sir ? "

"No," replied Dr. Spenlove, in a cheerful tone. "You are a stranger to me, as I have no doubt I am to you."

"You are not quite a stranger, sir," she said, timidly. "I have heard of your kindness to many suffering people."

"Tush, tush!" he exclaimed. "A man deserves no credit for doing his duty. You feel stronger now, do you not? If you have no doctor you must allow me to come and see you. Do not hesitate; you need such advice as I can give you; and," he added gently, "I will send in my account when you are rich. Not till then, upon my honour; and meanwhile I promise to ask no questions."

"I am deeply grateful to you, sir."

And, indeed, when they parted the world was a little brighter to the poor soul.

From that day he attended her regularly, and she was strengthened and comforted by his considerate conduct towards her. She was known as Mrs. Turner; but it was strange, if she were wife or widow, that she should wear no wedding-ring. As their intimacy ripened his first impression that she was a lady was confirmed, and although he was naturally curious about her history, he kept his promise by not asking her any questions which he instinctively felt it would be painful to her to answer. Even when he discovered that she was about to become a mother he made no inquiries concerning the father of her unborn child. On the day he bade her farewell, her baby, a girl, was two weeks old, and a dark and terrible future lay before the hapless woman. His heart bled for her, but he was powerless to help her further. Weak and despairing, she sat in her chair with her child at her wasted breast ; her dark and deep-sunken eyes seemed to be contemplating this future in hopeless terror.

" I am grieved to leave you so," he said, gazing sadly at her ; " but it is out of my power to do what I would wish. Unhappily, I am almost as poor as yourself. You will try to get strong, will you not ? "

" I don't know," she murmured.

" Remember," he said, taking her hand, " you have a duty to perform. What will you do when you are strong ? "

" I don't know."

" Nay, nay," he gently urged, " you must not speak so despondently. Believe me, I do not wish to force your confidence, but I have gathered from chance

words you have let drop that you lived in London.
I am going there to-morrow. Can I call upon any
person who would be likely to assist you?"

"There is no one."

"But surely you must have some friends or re-
lations——"

"I have none. When you leave me I shall be
without a friend in the world."

"God help you!" he sighed.

"Will He?"

The question was asked in the voice of one who
had abandoned hope, who had lost faith in human
goodness and eternal justice, and who was tasting
the bitterness of death.

Dr. Spenlove remained with her an hour, striving
to cheer her, to instil hope into her heart, but his
words had no effect upon her; and, indeed, he felt
at times that the platitudes to which he was giving
utterance were little better than mockery. Was
not this woman face to face with the practical issues
of life and death in their most awful aspect, and
was it not a stern fact that there was but one
practical remedy for them? She asked for bread,
and he was offering her a stone. It was then he
went from her room and learned the full truth

from her landlord, who was only waiting till he was gone to turn her into the streets. We know by what means he bought a day's respite for her. Finally he left her, and bore away with him the darkest picture of human misery of which he had ever had experience.

CHAPTER II.

HIS landlady, Mrs. Radcliffe, met him on the doorstep, and informed him that the gentleman who had called to see him in the afternoon had called again, and was in his room.

"A word, Mrs. Radcliffe," he said, hurriedly. "I am going to ask a great favour of you. I owe you two weeks' rent."

"Yes, sir."

His heart sank within him; he divined immediately from her tone that she was in need of the money.

"Would it inconvenience you to wait a little while for it?"

"I must, sir, if you haven't got it," she replied, "but I am dreadfully hard pressed, and I reckoned on it. I'm behindhand myself, sir, and my land-lord's been threatening me——"

"Say no more, Mrs. Radcliffe. Justice must be first served. I have the money; take it—for

16

Heaven's sake take it quickly! I must not rob the poor to help the poor."

He muttered the last words to himself as he thrust the sixteen shillings into her hand.

" I am so sorry, sir," said the distressed woman.

He interrupted her with, " There, there, I am ashamed that I asked you. I am sure no one has a kinder heart than you, and I am greatly obliged to you for all the attention you have shown me while I have been in your house. The gentleman is in my room, you say ? "

It was a proof of Mrs. Radcliffe's kindness of heart that there was a bright fire blazing in the room, made with her own coals, and that the lamp had been replenished with her own oil. Dr. Spenlove was grateful to her, and he inwardly acknowledged that he could not have otherwise disposed of the few shillings which he had no right to call his own. His visitor rose as he entered, a well-dressed man some forty years of age, sturdily built, with touches of grey already in his hair and beard, and with signs in his face and on his forehead indicative of a strong will.

" Dr. Spenlove ? " he asked, as they stood facing each other.

" That is my name."

" Mine is Gordon. I have come to see you on a matter of great importance."

Dr. Spenlove motioned to the chair from which his visitor had risen, and he resumed his seat ; but although he had said that he had come upon a matter of great importance, he seemed to be either in no hurry to open it, or to be uncertain in which way to do so, for he sat for some moments in silence, smoothing his bearded chin and studying Dr. Spenlove's face with a stern and studious intentness.

" Can you spare me half an hour of your time ? " he said at length.

" Longer, if you wish," said Dr. Spenlove.

" It may be longer, if you offer no opposition to the service I wish you to render me ; and perhaps it is as well to say that I am willing and can afford to pay for the service."

Dr. Spenlove bent his head.

" It is seldom," continued Mr. Gordon, " that I make mistakes, and the reason is not far to seek. I make inquiries, I clear the ground, I resolve upon a course of action, and I pursue it to its end without deviation. I will be quite frank with you, Dr. Spenlove ; I am a hard, inflexible man. Thrown upon the world when I was a lad, I pushed my way to fortune. I am self-made ; I can speak fair English. I have received little education, none at all in a classical way; but I possess common sense, and I make it apply to my affairs. That is better than education if a man is resolved to get along in life— as I was resolved to do. When I was a young man I said, ' I will grow rich, or I will know the reason why.' I have grown rich. I do not say it as a boast—it is only fools who boast—but I am worth to-day a solid twenty thousand pounds a year. I make this statement merely as a proof that I am in a position to carry out a plan in which I desire your assistance and co-operation."

" My dear sir," said Dr. Spenlove, who could not but perceive that his visitor was very much in earnest, " the qualities you mention are admirable in their way, but I fear you have come to the wrong man. I am a doctor, and if you do not need my professional advice——"

" Stop a moment," interrupted Mr. Gordon, " I have come to the right man, and I do not need professional advice. I am as sound as a bell, and I have never had occasion to pay a doctor's fee.

I know what I am about in the mission which brings me here. I have made inquiries concerning you, and have heard something of your career and its results; I have heard of your kindnesses and of the esteem in which you are held. You have influence with your patients; any counsel you might give them, apart from your prescriptions, would be received with respect and attention; and I believe I am not wrong when I say that you are to some extent a man of the world."

"To some slight extent only," corrected Dr. Spenlove, with a faint smile.

"Sufficient," proceeded Mr. Gordon, "for my purpose. You are not blind to the perils which lie before weak and helpless women—before, we will say, a woman who has no friends, who is living where she is not known, who is in a position of grave danger, who is entirely without means, who is young and good-looking, and who, at the best, is unable by the work of her hands to support herself."

Dr. Spenlove looked sharply at his visitor. "You have such a woman in your mind, Mr. Gordon."

"I have such a woman in my mind, Dr. Spenlove."

"A patient of mine?"

· " A patient of yours."

There was but one who answered to this description, and whose future was so dark and hopeless. For the first time during the interview he began to be interested in his visitor. He motioned him to proceed.

" We are speaking in confidence, Dr. Spenlove ? "

" In perfect confidence, Mr. Gordon."

" Whether my errand here is successful or not, I ask that nothing that passes between us shall ever be divulged to a third person."

" I promise it."

" I will mention the name of the woman to whom I have referred, or, it will be more correct to say, the name by which she is known to you. Mrs. Turner."

" You mean her no harm, sir ? "

" None. I am prepared to befriend her, to save her, if my conditions are accepted."

Dr. Spenlove drew a deep breath of relief. He would go to his new field of labours with a light heart if this unhappy woman were saved.

" You have come at a critical moment," he said, " and you have accurately described the position in which she is placed. But how can my mediation, or the mediation of any man, be necessary in such a case ? She will hail you as her saviour and the saviour of her babe. Hasten to her immediately, dear sir; or perhaps you do not know where she lives, and wish me to take you to her? I am ready. Do not let us lose a moment, for every moment deepens her misery."

He did not observe the frown which passed into Mr. Gordon's face at his mention of the child; he was so eager that his hat was already on his head and his hand on the handle of the door.

Mr. Gordon did not rise from his chair.

" You are in too great a hurry, Dr. Spenlove. Be seated, and listen to what I have to say. You ask how your mediation can avail. I answer, in the event of her refusal to accept the conditions upon which I am ready to marry her."

" To marry her! " exclaimed Dr. Spenlove.

" To marry her," repeated Mr. Gordon. " She is not a married woman, and her real name need not be divulged. When you hear the story I am about to relate, when you hear the conditions, the only conditions, upon which I will consent to lift her from the degraded depths into which she has fallen, you will understand why I desire your assistance. You will be able to make clear to her the effect of her consent or refusal upon her destiny and the destiny of her child; you will be able to use arguments which are in my mind, but to which I shall not give utterance. And remember, through all, that her child is a child of shame, and that I hold out to her the only prospect of that child being brought up in a reputable way and of herself being raised to a position of respectability."

He paused a moment or two before he opened fresh matter.

" I was a poor lad, Dr. Spenlove, without parents, without a home ; and when I was fourteen years of age I was working as an errand-boy in London, and keeping myself upon a wage of four shillings a week. I lost this situation through the bankruptcy of my employer, and I was not successful in obtaining another. One day, I saw on the walls a bill of a vessel going to Australia, and I applied at the agent's office with a vague idea that I might obtain a passage by working aboard ship in some capacity or other. I was a strong boy—starvation agrees with some lads— and a willing boy, and it happened that one of my stamp was wanted in the cook's galley. I was engaged at a shilling a month, and I landed in Melbourne with four shillings in my pocket.

" How I lived till I became a man is neither here

nor there ; but when gold was discovered I lived well,
for I got enough to buy a share in a cattle station
which now belongs entirely to me. In 1860, being
then on the high road to fortune, I made the
acquaintance of a man whom I will call Mr. Charles,
and of his only child, a girl of fourteen, whom I will
call Mary. I was taken with Mr. Charles, and I was
taken in by him as well, for he disappeared from the
colony a couple of years afterwards, in my debt to the
tune of a thousand pounds. He had the grace to
write to me from London, saying he would pay me
some day; and there the matter rested for seven
years more, which brings me to two years ago.

" At that time I had occasion to visit England on
business ; and in London I hunted up my debtor,
and we renewed our acquaintance. Mary was then
a young woman of twenty-one ; and had it not been
for her, it is more than likely I might have made
things unpleasant for her father, who was leading
the disreputable life of a gambler on racecourses, and
in clubs of a low character.

" Dr. Spenlove, you must have gathered from the
insight I have given you into my character that I am
not a man of sentiment, and you will probably consider it all the more strange that I should have

entertained feelings towards Mary which caused me
to consider whether she would not make me a credit-
able wife. Of these feelings I prefe not to speak in
a warmer strain, but shall leave you to place your
own construction upon them. While I was debating
with myself as to the course I should pursue, the
matter was decided for me by the death of Mr. Charles.
He died in disgrace and poverty, and Mary was left
friendless and homeless.

" I stepped in to her rescue, and I made a proposal
of marriage to her. At the same time, I told her that
I thought it advisable, for her sake and mine, that
a little time should elapse before this proposal was
carried into effect. I suggested that our marriage
should take place in two years ; meanwhile, I would
return to Australia, to build a suitable house and to
prepare a home for her, and she would remain in
England to fit herself for her new sphere of duties.
She accepted me, and I arranged with a lady of
refinement to receive her. To this lady both she and
I were utter strangers, and it was settled between
Mary and myself that she should enter her temporary
home under an assumed name. It was my proposal
that this pardonable deceit should be practised ; no
person was wronged by it, and it would assist towards

Mary's complete severance from old associations. Our future was in our own hands, and concerned nobody but ourselves.

"I returned to Australia, and made my preparations. We corresponded once a month, and some few months ago I informed her of the date of my intended arrival in England. To that letter I received no reply ; and when I landed and called at the lady's house, I learned that she had fled. I set to work to discover the truth, and I have discovered it ; I set to work to track her, and I have succeeded. Her story is a common story of betrayal and desertion, and I am not inclined to trouble you with it. She has not the remotest hope of assistance from the man who betrayed her ; she has not the remotest hope of assistance from a person in the world with the exception of myself.

"Dr. Spenlove, notwithstanding what has occurred I am here in Portsmouth this night with the intention of carrying out the engagement into which I entered with her ; I am here, prepared to marry her, on express conditions. The adoption of assumed names, the obscurity she has courted, the absolute silence which is certain to be observed by her, by me, by you, by the man who betrayed her, render me safe. It is known that I have come to England to be married, and she will be accepted as I present her when I return with her as my wife. I will have no discussion as to my motives for taking what the world would consider an unwise step ; but you will understand that my feelings for the woman who has played me false must be of a deep and sincere nature, or I should not dream of taking it.

"It now only remains for me to state the conditions under which I am prepared to save her from even a more shameful degradation than that into which she has already fallen. I speak plainly. You know as well as I the fate that is in store for her if my offer is rejected."

CHAPTER III.

MR. GORDON had spoken throughout in a cold, passionless tone, and with no accent of emotion in his voice. If anything could have been destructive of the idea that he loved the woman he wished to marry, it was his measured delivery of the story he had related ; and yet there could be no question that there was some nobility in the nature of the sacrifice he was prepared to make for her sake. The contrast between the man and the woman struck Dr. Spenlove very forcibly. The man was hard and cold, the woman was sensitive and sympathetic. Had their circumstances been equal, and had Dr. Spenlove been an interested adviser, he would have had no hesitation in saying to her : "Do not marry this man : there is no point of union between you ; you can never kindle in his heart the fire which burns within your own ; wedded to him, a dull routine of years will be your portion."

28

But he felt that he dared not encourage himself to pursue this line of argument. Although the most pregnant part of Mr. Gordon's errand had yet to be disclosed, it seemed to him that he would very likely presently be the arbiter of her destiny. "You will be able," Mr. Gordon had said, "to make clear to her the effect of her consent or refusal upon her destiny and the destiny of her child." Whatever the conditions, it would be his duty to urge her to accept the offer that would be made to her ; otherwise, he might be condemning her to a course of life he shuddered to contemplate. The responsibility would be too solemn for mere sentimental consideration. These were the thoughts that flashed through his mind in the momentary pause before Mr. Gordon spoke again.

"I believe," his visitor then said, "that I am in possession of the facts relating to Mrs. Turner"— he reverted to the name by which she was generally known—"but you will corroborate them perhaps. She is in want."

"She is in the lowest depths of poverty."

"Unless she pays the arrears of rent she will be turned into the streets to-morrow."

"That is the landlord's determination."

"She would have been turned out to-day but for your intervention."

"You are well informed, I see," observed Dr. Spenlove, rather nettled.

"I have conversed with the landlord and with others concerning her. She lives among the poor, who have troubles enough of their own to grapple with, and are unable, even if they were inclined, to render her the assistance of which she stands in need. She seems to have kept herself aloof from them, for which I commend her. Now, Dr. Spenlove, I will have no spectre of shame and degradation to haunt her life and mine. Her past must be buried, and the grave must never be opened To that I am resolved, and no power on earth can turn me from it."

"But her child?" faltered Dr. Spenlove.

"She will have no child. She must part with her, and the parting must be final and irrevocable. The steps I shall take to this end shall be so effectual that if by chance in the future they should happen to meet there shall be no possibility of recognition. I propose to have the child placed with a family who will adopt her as a child of their own—there will be little difficulty in finding such a family—to the head of which a sum of one hundred pounds will be paid yearly for maintenance. I name no limit as to time; so long as the child lives, so long will the payment be made through my lawyers. Should the child die before she reaches the age of twenty-one, the sum of five hundred pounds will be paid to the people who undertake the charge. They will know nothing of me or of the mother; our names will not be divulged to them, and they will not be able to trace us. Should they evince a disposition to be troublesome in this respect, the child will be taken from them by my lawyers, and another home provided for her. A hundred pounds a year is a liberal sum, and there will not be the least difficulty in carrying out the proposed arrangement. In proof that I desire the child to have every chance of leading a happy life, I will engage to give her a marriage portion of five hundred pounds. Judge for yourself whether a woman in Mrs. Turner's circumstances would be acting wisely in rejecting my proposition."

"You have spoken in a most generous spirit," said Dr. Spenlove slowly, "so far as money goes; but you seem not to have taken into consideration a mother's feelings."

"I have not taken them into consideration: they are not part of my plan. I have looked at the matter only from two points of view—its worldly aspect, and my desire to carry out my personal wishes. I decline to regard it or to argue upon it from the point of view of a mother's feelings. I ask you to judge of it as a man of the world."

"Of which," said Dr. Spenlove, "as I have hinted to you, I am a poor example. Do you expect me to provide for the babe such a home as that you have described?"

"Not at all. It is my business to carry out my plan if she accepts the conditions."

"What, then, do you wish me to do?"

"To lay my proposition before her as nearly as possible in my words, to impress upon her that it is her duty to agree to it, for her own sake and for the sake of the child."

"Why not do so yourself?"

"I have not seen her; I will not see her while she holds in her arms her burden of shame. She shall come to me free and unencumbered, or she shall not come at all. I could not speak to her as I have spoken to you; I should not be able to command myself. She would plead to me, and I should answer her in bitterness and anger. Such a scene would set me so strongly against her that I should immediately relinquish my purpose. You can reason with her; you can show her the path in which her duty clearly lies. I do not deny that she is called upon to make a sacrifice; but it is a sacrifice which will lead to good, it is a sacrifice which every right-minded man would urge her to make. Indifferent man of the world as you proclaim yourself to be, you cannot be blind to the almost sure fate in store for her in the circumstances in which she is placed. Your experiences must have made you acquainted with the stories of women who have fallen as she has fallen, and you will know how many of them were raised from the depths, and how many of them fell into deeper shame. Dr. Spenlove, I have entirely finished what I came here to say."

"Before I undertake to do what you require of me," said Dr. Spenlove, who by this time understood the man he had to deal with, "I must ask you a question or two."

"If they relate to the present business," responded Mr. Gordon, "I will answer them."

"Failing me, will you employ some other person to act as your envoy to Mrs. Turner?"

"I shall employ no other, for the reason that there is no other whose counsel would be likely to influence her. And for another reason—I have disclosed to you what I will disclose to no other person."

"Would you leave her as she is?"

"I would leave her as she is. Early in the morning I should take my departure, and she would have to face the future unaided by me."

"If she will not listen to me, if she will not make the sacrifice, you will surely give her out of your abundance some little assistance to help her along?"

"Out of my abundance," replied Mr. Gordon, sternly, "I will give her nothing—not the smallest coin. Make your mind easy upon one point, Dr. Spenlove. So far as a practical man like myself is likely to go, I will do what I can to make her happy if she affords me the opportunity. She will live in a respectable atmosphere, she will be surrounded by respectable people, she will have all the comforts that money can purchase, and I shall never utter to her a word of reproach. Her past will be as dead to me as if it had never been."

Dr. Spenlove rose. "It is your desire that I shall go to her to-night?"

"It is. The matter must be settled without delay."

"If she asks for time to reflect——"

"I must have an answer to-night, yea or nay."

There was no more to be said. The man who had been wronged and deceived, and who had made an offer so strange, and generous, and cruel, was fixed and implacable.

"I may be absent some time," said Dr. Spenlove. "Where shall I see you upon my return?"

"Here, if you will allow me to stay."

"You are welcome. My landlady will make you a bed on the sofa."

"Thank you; I need no bed. I can employ myself while you are away."

Dr. Spenlove stepped to the door, and turned on the threshold.

"One other question, Mr. Gordon. If I succeed, when will you require her to give up her child?"

"To-morrow evening. I will have a carriage ready at the door. On the following day Mrs. Turner and I will leave Portsmouth, and there is no probability, after that, that you and I will ever meet again."

Dr. Spenlove nodded, and left the house.

CHAPTER IV.

FLIGHT.

THE snow was falling more heavily, and a strong wind blew the flakes into his face as he made his way to Mrs. Turner's garret. He walked as quickly as he could, but his progress was impeded by the force of the wind and by its driving the snow into his eyes. Despite these obstacles he preserved his mental balance, and was observant of all that was passing around him ; and it was a proof of his kindly and unselfish nature that, in the light of the vital errand upon which he was engaged, he was oblivious of the sense of physical discomfort. Conflicting questions agitated his mind. No longer under the influence of the cold, cruel logic which distinguished Mr. Gordon's utterances, he once more asked himself whether he would be acting rightly in urging Mrs. Turner to renounce her maternal duties and obligations, and to part for ever with the child of her blood. The human and the Divine law were in conflict.

36

On one side degradation and direst poverty from which there seemed no prospect of escape, and driving the mother perhaps to a course of life condemned alike by God and man ; on the other side a life of material comfort and respectability for herself and her child. A fortuitous accident—a chance for which he had prayed earlier in the night—had made him at once the arbiter and the judge ; his hand was on the wheel to steer these two helpless beings through the voyage upon which they were embarked, and upon him rested the responsibility of their future. There was no case here of ploughing through unknown waters over hidden rocks ; he saw the ocean of life before him, he saw the rocks beneath. Amid those rocks lay the forms of lost abandoned women who in their mortal career would surely have been saved had an offer of rescue come, such as had come to the woman who chiefly occupied his thoughts. They would have been spared the suffering of despairing days, the horrors of a despairing death ; they would have been lifted from the gulf of shame and ignominy. New hopes, new joys would have arisen to comfort them. The sacrifice they would have been called upon to make would have been hallowed by the consciousness that they had performed their duty.

It was not alone the happiness of the mortal life that had to be considered ; if the ministrations of God's ministers on earth were not a mockery and a snare, it was the immortal life that was equally at stake. The soul's reward sprang from the body's suffering.

And still the pitiless snow fell, and the wind howled around him ; and through the white whirlwind he beheld the light of heaven and the stars shining upon him.

How should he act? He imagined himself steering the vessel through an ocean of sad waters. On the right lay a haven of rest, on the left lay a dark and desolate shore. Here, salvation ; there, destruction. Which way should he turn the wheel? His pity for her had drawn from him during their last interview the exclamation, " God help you ! " and she had asked hopelessly, " Will He? " He had turned from her then ; he had no answer to make. There is, he said to himself now, no Divine mediation in human affairs ; the Divine hand is not stretched forth to give food to the hungry. In so grave an issue as the starvation of a human being, dependence upon Divine aid will not avail. Admitting this, he felt it to be almost a heresy, but at the same time he knew that it was true.

There were but few people in the white streets, and of those few a large proportion tinged his musings with a deeper melancholy. These were ragged shivering children, and women recklessly or despondently gashing the white carpet, so pure and innocent and fair in its sentimental, so hard and bitter and cruel in its material aspect. By a devious process of reasoning he drew a parallel between it and the problem he was engaged in solving. It was poetic, and it freezed the marrow ; it had a soul and a body, one a sweet and smiling spirit, the other a harsh and frowning reality. The heart of a poet without boots would have sunk within him as he trod the snow-clad streets.

Dr. Spenlove's meditations were arrested by a sudden tumult. A number of people approached him, gesticulating and talking eagerly and excitedly, the cause of their excitement being a couple of policemen who bore between them the wet limp body of a motionless woman. He was drawn magnetically towards the crowd, and was immediately recognised.

" Here's Dr. Spenlove," they cried ; " he knows her."

Yes, he knew her the moment his eyes fell upon

her, the people having made way for him. The
body borne by the policeman was that of a young
girl scarcely out of her teens, an unfortunate who
had walked the streets for two or three years past.

"You had better come with us, doctor," said one
of the policemen, to both of whom he was known.
"We have just picked her out of the water."

A middle-aged woman pushed herself close to Dr.
Spenlove.

"She said she'd do it a month ago," said this
woman, "if luck didn't turn."

Good God! If luck didn't turn! What direction
in the unfortunate girl's career was the lucky turn to
take to prevent her from courting death?

"You will come with us, sir?" said the policeman.

"Yes," answered Dr. Spenlove, mechanically.

The police station was but a hundred yards away,
and thither they walked, Dr. Spenlove making a
hasty examination of the body as they proceeded.

"Too late, I'm afraid, sir," said the policeman.

"I fear so," said Dr. Spenlove, gravely.

It proved to be the case. The girl was dead.

The signing of papers and other formalities detained
Dr. Spenlove at the police station for nearly an hour,
and he departed with a heavy weight at his heart.

He had been acquainted with the girl whose life's troubles were over since the commencement of his career in Portsmouth. She was then a child of fourteen, living with her parents, who were respectable working people. Growing into dangerous beauty, she had fallen as others had fallen, and had fled from her home, to find herself after a time deserted by her betrayer. Meanwhile the home in which she had been reared was broken up; the mother died, the father left the town. Thrown upon her own resources, she drifted into the ranks of the "unfortunates," and became a familiar figure in low haunts, one of civilisation's painted, bedizened night-birds of the streets. Dr. Spenlove had befriended her, counselled her, warned her, urged her to reform, and her refrain was, "What can I do? I must live." It was not an uncommon case; the good doctor came in contact with many such, and could have prophesied with unerring accuracy the fate in store for them. The handwriting is ever on the wall, and no special gift is needed to decipher it. Drifting, drifting, drifting, for ever drifting and sinking lower and lower till the end comes. It had come soon to this young girl— mercifully, thought Dr. Spenlove, as he plodded slowly on, for surely the snapping of life's chord in the springtime of her life was better than the sure descent into a premature haggard and sinful old age. Recalling these reminiscences, his doubts with respect to his duty in the mission he had undertaken were solved. There was but one safe course for Mrs. Turner to follow.

He hastened his steps. His interview with Mr. Gordon and the tragic incident in which he had been engaged had occupied a considerable time, and it was now close upon midnight. It was late for an ordinary visit, but he was a medical man, and the doors of his patients were open to him at all hours. In the poor neighbourhood in which Mrs. Turner resided, many of the street-doors were left unlocked night and day for the convenience of the lodgers, and her house being one of these, Dr. Spenlove had no difficulty in obtaining admission. He shook the snow from his clothes, and, ascending the stairs, knocked at Mrs. Turner's door ; no answer coming he knocked again and again, and at length he turned the handle and entered.

The room was quite dark ; there was no fire in the grate, no candle alight. He listened for the sound of breathing, but none reached his ears.

" Mrs. Turner ! " he cried.

Receiving no response he struck a match, and looked around. The room was empty. Greatly alarmed he went to the landing, and knocked at an adjoining door. A woman's voice called,—

" Who's there ? "

" It is I, Dr. Spenlove."

" Wait a moment, sir."

He heard shuffling steps, and presently the tenant appeared, only partially dressed, with a lighted candle in her hand.

" I didn't send for you, doctor," she said.

" No. I want to ask you about Mrs. Turner. She is not in her room."

" I thought it was strange I didn't hear the baby crying, but I don't know where she is."

" Did you not hear her go out ? "

" No, sir ; I came home at ten soaked through and through, and I was glad to get to bed. It ain't a night a woman would care to keep out in unless she couldn't help herself."

" Indeed it is not. Did you see anything of her before you went to bed ? "

" I didn't see her, I heard her. I was just going off when she knocked at my door, and asked if I could give her a little milk for the baby ; but I hadn't any to give. Besides, she ain't got a feeding-bottle that I know of. She's been trying to borrow one, but nobody in the house could oblige her. She's having a hard time of it, doctor."

" She is, poor soul!" said Dr. Spenlove, with a sigh.

" It's the way with all of us, sir; no one ought to know that better than you do. There ain't a lodger in the house that's earning more than twelve shillings a week; not much to keep a family on, is it, sir? And we've got a landlord with a heart of stone. If it hadn't been for her baby, and that it might have got him in hot water, he'd have turned her out weeks ago. He's bound to do it to-morrow if her rent ain't paid. He told me so this morning when he screwed the last penny out of me."

" Do you know whether she succeeded in obtaining milk for the child?"

" It's hardly likely, I should say. Charity begins at home, doctor."

" It is natural and just that it should; but it is terrible, terrible! Where can Mrs. Turner have gone to?"

" Heaven knows. One thing I do know, doctor, she's got no friends; she wouldn't make any, kept

herself to herself, gave herself airs, some said, though
I don't go as far as that. I dare say she has her
reasons, only when a woman sets herself up like that
it turns people against her. Are you sure she ain't
in her room?"

"The room is empty."

"It's enough to be the death of a baby to take it
out such a night as this. Listen to the wind."

A furious gust shook the house, and made every
window rattle. To Dr. Spenlove's agitated senses it
seemed to be alive with ominous voices, proclaiming
death and destruction to every weak and helpless
creature that dared to brave it. He passed his hand
across his forehead in distress.

"I must find her. I suppose you cannot tell me
of any place she may have gone to for assistance?"

"I can't, sir. There's a bare chance that as she
had no coals and no money to buy 'em with, some
one in the house has taken her in for the night. I'll
inquire, if you like."

"I shall be obliged to you if you will," said Dr.
Spenlove, catching eagerly at the suggestion; "and I
pray that you may be right."

"You won't mind waiting in the passage, sir, till
I've dressed myself. I sha'n't be a minute."

She was very soon ready, and she went about the house making inquiries ; and, returning, said that none of the lodgers could give her any information concerning Mrs. Turner.

" I am sorry to have disturbed you," said Dr. Spenlove ; and, wishing her good-night, he once more faced the storm. The fear by which he was oppressed was that the offer of succour had come too late, and that Mrs. Turner had been driven by despair to the execution of some desperate design to put an end to her misery. Instinctively, and with a sinking heart, he took the direction of the sea, hurrying eagerly after every person he saw ahead of him, in the hope that it might be the woman of whom he was in search. The snow was many inches thick on the roads, and was falling fast ; the wind tore through the now almost deserted streets, moaning, sobbing, shrieking, with an appalling human suggestion in its tones created by Dr. Spenlove's fears. Now and then he met a policeman, and stopped to exchange a few words with him, the intention of which was to ascertain if the man had seen any person answering to the description of Mrs. Turner. He did not mention her by name, for he had an idea—supposing his search to be happily successful—that Mr. Gordon would withdraw his offer if any publicity were attracted to the woman he was ready to marry. The policemen could not assist him; they had seen no woman with a baby in her arms tramping the streets on this wild night.

"Anything special, sir?" they asked.

"No," he replied, "nothing special;" and so went on his way.

CHAPTER V.

DEATH BETTER THAN LIFE.

WHEN Dr. Spenlove left Mrs. Turner she sat for
some time in a state of dull lethargy. No tear
came into her eyes, no sigh escaped from her bosom.
During the past few months she had exhausted the
entire range of remorseful and despairing emotion.
The only comfort she had received through all
those dreary months sprang from the helpful sympathy of Dr. Spenlove; apart from that she had never
been buoyed up by a ray of light, had never been
cheered by the hope of a brighter day. Her one
prevailing thought was that she would be better
dead than alive. She did not court death; she
waited for it, and silently prayed that it would
come soon. It was not from the strength of inward
moral support that she had the courage to live
on; it was simply that she had schooled herself
into the belief that before or when her child was
born death would release her from the horrors of

life. Young as she was she so fostered this hope that it became a conviction, and she looked forward to the end with dull resignation. "If I live till my baby is born," she thought, "I pray that it may die with me."

Here was the case of a woman without the moral support which springs from faith in any kind of religion. In some few mortals such faith is intuitive, but in most instances it requires guidance and wise direction in childhood. Often it degenerates into bigotry and intolerance, and assumes the hateful narrow form of condemning to perdition all who do not subscribe to its own particular creed· Pagans are as worthy of esteem as the bigots who arrogate to themselves the monopoly of heavenly rewards.

Mrs. Turner was neither pagan nor bigot; she was a nullity. Her religious convictions had not yet taken shape, and though, if she had been asked, "Are you a Christian?" she would have replied, "Oh yes, I am a Christian," she would have been unable to demonstrate in what way she was a Christian, or what she understood by the term. In this respect many thousands of human beings resemble her.

Faith is strength, mightier than the sword, mightier than the pen, mightier than all the world's store of gold and precious stones ; and when this strength is displayed in the sweetness of resignation, and in submission to the Divine will which chastens human life with sorrow, its influence upon the passions is sustaining, and purifying, and sublime· If Mrs. Turner had been blessed with faith which displayed itself in this direction, she would have been the happier for it, and hard as were her trials, she would to the last have looked forward with hope instead of despair.

The story related by Mr. Gordon to Dr. Spenlove was true in every particular. There was no distortion or exaggeration ; he had done for Mrs. Turner and her father all that he said he had done. He had not mentioned the word "love" in connection with the woman he had asked to be his wife. She, on her part, had no such love for him as that which should bind a man and a woman in a life-long tie ; she held him in respect and esteem —that was all. But she had accepted him, and had contemplated the future with satisfaction until, until——

Until a man crossed her path who wooed her

in different fashion, and who lavished upon her flatteries and endearments which made her false to the promise she had given. For this man she had deserted the home which Mr. Gordon had provided for her, and had deserted it in such a fashion that she could never return to it, could never again be received in it, and this without a word of explanation to the man she had deceived. She was in her turn deceived, and she awoke from her dream to find herself a lost and abandoned woman. In horror she fled from him, and cast her lot among strangers, knowing full well that she would meet with unbearable contumely among those to whom she was known. Hot words had passed between her and her betrayer, and in her anger she had written letters to him which in the eyes of the law would have released him from any obligation it might otherwise have imposed upon him. He was well pleased with this, and he smiled as he put those letters in a place of safety—to be brought forward only in case she annoyed him. She did nothing of the kind; her scorn for him was so profound that she was content to release him unconditionally. So she passed out of his life as he passed out of hers. Neither of these beings, the betrayed or the betrayer, reckoned with the future; neither of them gave a thought to the probability that the skeins of Fate, which to-day separated them as surely as if they had lived at opposite poles of the earth, might at some future time bring them together again, and that the pages of the book which they believed was closed for ever might be reopened for weal or woe.

The child's moans aroused the mother from her lethargy. She had no milk to give the babe; nature's founts were dry, and she went from door to door in the house in which she lived to beg for food. She returned as she went, empty-handed, and the child continued to moan.

Dr. Spenlove, her only friend, had bidden her farewell. She had not a penny in her pocket; there was not a crust of bread in the cupboard, not an ounce of coal, not a stick of wood to kindle a fire. She was thinly clad, and she did not possess a single article upon which she could have obtained the smallest advance. She had taken the room furnished, but even if what it contained had been her property a broker would have given but a few shillings for everything in it.

The little hand instinctively wandered to the

mother's wasted breast, and plucked at it imploringly, ravenously. The woman looked around in the last throes of an anguish too deep for expression, except in the appalling words to which she gave despairing utterance.

"Come," she cried, "we will end it!"

Out into the cold streets she crept, unobserved. She shivered, and a pitiful smile crossed her lips.

"Hush, hush!" she murmured to her babe. "It will soon be over. Better dead—better dead—for you and for me!"

She crept towards the sea, and hugged the wall when she heard approaching footsteps. She need not have feared; the night was too inclement for any but selfish consideration. The soft snow fell, and enwrapped her and her child in its pitiless shroud. She paused by a lamp-post, and cast an upward look at the heavens, in which she could see the glimmering of the stars. Then she went on, and fretfully pressed her babe close to her breast, to stifle the feeble sobs.

"Be still, be still!" she murmured. "There is no hope in life for either of us. Better dead—better dead!"

CHAPTER VI.

THE FRIEND IN NEED.

DESPERATELY resolved as she was to carry her fatal design into execution she had not reckoned with nature. Weakened by the life of privation she had led for so many months, and also by the birth of her child, her physical forces had reached the limit of human endurance. She faltered and staggered, the ground slipped from beneath her weary feet. Vain was the struggle, her vital power was spent. From her overcharged heart a voiceless and terrible prayer went up to heaven. "Give me strength, O God, give me but a little strength! I have not far to go!" She fought the air with her disengaged hand, and tossed her head this way and that; but her ruthless prayer was not answered, and though she struggled fiercely she managed to crawl only a few more steps. She had yet hundreds of yards to go to reach the sea when some chord within her seemed to snap; her farther progress was instantly arrested, and she found herself incapable of moving backward or forward. Swaying to and fro, the earth, the sky, the whirling snow, and the dim light of the stars swam in her sight and faded from before her. In that supreme moment she saw a spiritual vision of her dishonoured life. Deprived early of a mother's counsel and companionship, she had passed her days with a spendthrift father, whose love for her was so tainted with selfishness that it was not only valueless, but mischievous. When she grew to woman's estate she was worse than alone ; she had no guide, no teacher, to point out the rocks and shoals of maiden-hood, to inculcate in her the principles of virtue which would act as a safeguard against the specious wiles of men whose eyes were charmed by her beauty, and whose only aim was to lure her to ruin. Then her father died, and a friend came forward who offered her a home and an honourable position in the world. Friendless and penniless, she accepted him, and gave him her promise, and accepted his money. Love had not touched her heart ; she thought it had when a wilier man wooed her in another and more alluring fashion, and by this man she had been beguiled and betrayed. Then she knew what she had lost, but it was too late ; her good name was gone, and she fled to a strange part

of the country and lived among strangers, a heart-
_broken, despairing woman. All the salient features
in her career flashed before her. She saw the man
who had trusted her, she saw the man in whom she
put her trust, she saw herself, an abandoned creature,
with a child of shame in her arms. These ghostly
figures stood clearly limned in that one last moment
of swiftly fading light, as in the moment of sunrise
on a frosty morning every distant object stands
sharply outlined against the sky ; then darkness fell
upon her, and with an inarticulate, despairing cry,
she sank to the ground in a deathlike swoon. The
wind sobbed and shrieked and wailed around her
and her child ; the falling snow, with treacherous
tenderness, fell softly upon them ; herself insensible,
she had no power to shake it off; her babe was
conscious, but its feeble movements were of small
avail against the white pall which was descending
upon it and its outcast mother. Thicker and
thicker it grew, and in the wild outcry of this bitter
night Fate seemed to have pronounced its inexorable
sentence of death against these unfortunate beings.

Ignorant of the fact that chance or a spiritual
messenger was guiding him aright, Dr. Spenlove
plodded through the streets. He had no clue, and

received none from the half-dozen persons or so he
encountered as he walked towards the sea. He was
scarcely fit for the task he had undertaken, but so
intent was he upon his merciful mission that he
bestowed no thought upon himself. The nipping
air aggravating the cough from which he was suffering, he kept his mouth closed as a protection, and
peered anxiously before him for some signs of the
woman he was pursuing. A man walked briskly
and cheerily towards him, puffing at a large and
fragrant cigar, and stamping his feet sturdily into
the snow. This man wore a demonstratively furred
overcoat ; his hands were gloved in fur ; his boots
were thick and substantial ; and in the independent
assertion that he was at peace with the world, and
on exceedingly good terms with himself, he hummed
the words, in Italian, of the Jewel Song in " Faust "
every time he removed the cigar from his lips.
Although it was but a humming reminiscence of the
famous and beautiful number, his faint rendering of
it was absolutely faultless, and proved him to be a
man of refined musicianly taste, quite out of keeping
with his demonstratively furred overcoat. Music,
however, was not his profession ; the instincts of his
race and a youthful ambition had welded the divine

art into his soul, and the instincts of his race had made him—a pawnbroker. Singular conjunction of qualities—the music of the celestial spheres and fourpence in the pound a month! A vulgar occupation, that of a pawnbroker, which high-toned gentlemen and mortals of aristocratic birth regard with scorn and contempt. But the last vulgar and debasing music-hall ditty which was carolled with delight by the majority of these gilded beings of a higher social grade never found lodgment in the soul of Mr. Moss, which, despite that he devoted his business hours to the lending of insignificant sums of money upon any small articles which were submitted to his judgment across the dark counter of his pawnbroking establishment, was attuned to a far loftier height than theirs in the divine realms of song. Puff, puff, puff at his cigar, the curling wreaths from which were whirled into threads of fantastic confusion by the gusts of wind, or hung in faint grey curls of beauty during a lull. The starry gleam was transferred from the lips to the fur-covered hand :—

> " E' strano poter il viso suo veder;
> Ah! mi posso guardar mi pospo rimirar.
> Di, sei tu ? Margherita !
> Di, sei tu? Dimmi su ;
> Dimmi su, di su, di su, di su presto ! "

From hand to lips the starry gleam, and the soul of Mr. Moss followed the air as he puffed his weed. . . .

> " E la figlia d'un re ! . . .
> Proseguiam l'adornamento.
> Vo provare ancor se mi stan
> Lo smaniglia ed il monil ! "

The pawnbroker broke into ecstasy. From lips to hand again the starry light, and his voice grew rapturous :—

> "Ciel ! E come una man
> Che sul baaccio mi posa !
> Ah ! Io rido in poter
> Me stessa qui veder ! "

The last trill brought him close to Dr. Spenlove.

" Friend, friend ! " cried the doctor. " A word with you, for charity's sake ! "

Mr. Moss did not disregard the appeal. Slipping off his right glove, and thereby displaying two fingers decorated with massive rings studded with diamonds, he fished a couple of coppers from a capacious pocket, and thrust them into Dr. Spenlove's outstretched palm. He thought it was a homeless beggar who had besought charity. Dr. Spenlove caught his hand, and said,—

" No, no, it is not for that. Will you kindly tell me——"

" Why," interrupted Mr. Moss, " it is Dr. Spenlove ! "

" Mr. Moss," said Dr. Spenlove, with a sigh of relief, " I am glad it is you, I am glad it is you."

" Not gladder than I am," responded Mr. Moss, jovially. " Even in weather like this I shouldn't care to be anybody else but myself."

This feeble attempt at humour was lost upon Dr. Spenlove.

" You have come from the direction I am taking, and you may have seen a person I am looking for—a woman with a baby in her arms, a poor woman, Mr. Moss, whom I am most anxious to find."

" I've come from the Hard, but I took no account of the people I passed. A man has enough to do to look after himself, with the snow making icicles in his hair, and the wind trying to bite his nose off his face. The first law of nature, you know, doctor, is—— "

" Humanity," interrupted Dr. Spenlove.

" No, no, doctor," corrected Mr. Moss ; "number one's the first law—number one, number one."

" You did not meet the woman, then ? "

· " Not to notice her. You've a bad cough, doctor ;

you'll have to take some of your own medicine."
He laughed. "Standing here is enough to freeze one."

"I am sorry I troubled you," said Dr. Spenlove,
hurt by the tone in which Mr. Moss spoke.
"Good-night."

He was moving away, when Mr. Moss detained
him.

"But look here, doctor, you're not fit to be
tramping the streets in this storm ; you ought to
be snuggled up between the blankets. Come home
with me, and Mrs. Moss shall make you a hot grog."

Dr. Spenlove shook his head, and passed on.
Mr. Moss gazed at the retreating figure, his thoughts
commingling.

" A charitable man, the good doctor, a large-hearted
gentleman. . . .

> 'Tardi si fa ahdio !
> Ah ! ti scongiuro invan.'

And poor as a church mouse. What woman is
he running after? Mrs. Moss would give her a
piece of her mind for taking out a baby on such
a night.

> ' Notte d'amor, tutta splendor,
> Begli astra d'oro.
> O celeste voluttà !
> Udir si, t'amo, t'adoro ! '

Too bad to let him go alone, such a good fellow
as he is; but Mrs. Moss will be waiting up for
me. . . . She won't mind when I tell her. . . . I've
a good mind to—yes, I will."

And after the doctor went Mr. Moss, and caught
up to him.

"Doctor, can I be of any assistance to you?"

"I shall be glad of your help," said Dr. Spenlove,
eagerly. "I'm rather worn out; I have had a
hard day."

"It's a trying life, the life of a doctor," said
Mr. Moss, sympathetically, as they walked slowly
on, side by side. "We were talking of it at home
only a month ago, when we were discussing what
we should put Michael to, our eldest boy, doctor."

"You have a large family," observed Dr. Spenlove.

"Not too large," said Mr. Moss, cheerfully. "Only
eleven. My mother had twenty-five, and I've a
sister with eighteen. Our youngest—what a rogue
he is, doctor!—is eight months; our eldest, Michael,
is seventeen next birthday. School days over, he
buckles to for work. We had a family council
to decide what he should be. We discussed all
the professions, and reduced them to two—doctor,
stockbroker. Michael had a leaning to be a doctor

—that's why we kept it in for discussion—but we succeeded in arguing him out of it. Your time's not your own, you see. Called up at all hours of the night, and in all weathers ; go to a dinner-party, and dragged away before it's half over, obliged to leave the best behind you ; can't enjoy a game of cards or billiards. You've got a little bet on, perhaps, or you're playing for points and have got a winning hand, when it's ' Doctor, you must come at once ; so-and-so's dying.' What's the consequence? You make a miscue, or you revoke, and you lose your money. If you're married, you're worse off than if you're single ; you haven't any comfort of your life. ' No, no, Michael,' says I, ' no doctoring. Stockbroking—that's what you'll go for.' And that's what he *is* going for. Most of our people, doctor, are lucky in their children. They don't forget to honour their father and their mother, that their days may be long in the land, and so on. There's big fish on the Stock Exchange, and they're worth trying for. What's the use of sprats ? It takes a hundred to fill a dish. Catch one salmon, and your dish is filled. A grand fish, doctor, a grand fish! What to do with your sons? Why, put them where they can make money ; don't make

scavengers or coal-heavers of them. *We* know what
we're about. There's no brain in the world to
compare with ours, and that's no boast, let me tell
you. Take your strikes, now. A strike of brick-
layers for a rise of twopence a day in their wages.
How many of our race among the strikers? Not
one. Did you ever see a Jewish bricklayer carrying
a hod up a hundred-foot ladder, and risking his
neck for bread, cheese, and beer? No, and you
never will. We did our share of that kind of work
in old Egypt ; we made all the bricks we wanted to,
and now we're taking a rest. A strike of bootmakers.
How many of our race among the cobblers? One
in a thousand, and he's an addlepate. We deal
in boots wholesale ; but we don't make them ourselves. Not likely. We send consignments of them
to the colonies, and open a dozen shops in every
large city, with fine plate-glass windows. We build
houses with *our* money and *your* bricks and mortar.
When we're after birds we don't care for sparrows :
we aim at eagles, and we bring them down ; we
bring them down." He beat his gloved hands
together, and chuckled. "What's your opinion,
doctor?"

"You are right, quite right," said Dr. Spenlove,

upon whose ears his companion's words had fallen like the buzzing of insects.

" Should say I was," said Mr. Moss. " I ought to have gone on the Stock Exchange myself; but when I was a young man I fancied I had a voice ; so I went in for music, studied Italian and all the famous operas till I knew them by heart almost, and found out in the end that my voice wasn't good enough. It was a great disappointment, because I had dreamt of making a fortune as a tenor. Signor Mossini—that was to be my name. My money being all spent, I had to take what was offered to me, a situation with a pawnbroker. That is how I became one, and I've no reason to regret it. Eh ? Why are you running away ? "

For Dr. Spenlove suddenly left his companion, and hurried forward.

During the time that Mr. Moss was unbosoming himself they had not met a soul, and Dr. Spenlove had seen nothing to sustain his hope of finding Mrs. Turner. But now his observant eyes detected a movement in the snow-laden road which thrilled him with apprehension, and caused him to hasten to the spot. It was as if some living creature were striving feebly to release itself from the fatal white

shroud.   Mr. Moss hurried after him, and they
reached the spot at the same moment.   In a fever
of anxiety Dr. Spenlove knelt and pushed the snow
aside, and then there came into view a baby's hand
and arm.

"Good God!" he murmured, and gently lifted
the babe from the cold bed.

"Is it alive? is it alive?" cried Mr. Moss, all
his nerves tingling with excitement.   "Give it to
me—quick! there's some one else there."

He saw portions of female clothing in the snow
which Dr. Spenlove was pushing frantically away.
He snatched up the babe, and, opening his fur coat,
clasped the little one to his breast, and enveloped
it in its warm folds.   Meanwhile Dr. Spenlove was
working at fever-heat.   To release Mrs. Turner
from her perilous position, to raise her to her feet,
to put his mouth to her mouth, his ear to her
heart, to assure himself there was a faint pulsation
in her body—all this was the work of a few
moments.

"Does she breathe, doctor?" asked Mr. Moss.

"She does," replied Dr. Spenlove; and added,
in deep distress, "but she may die in my arms."

"Not if we can save her.   Here, help me off with

this thick coat. Easy, easy; I have only one arm free. Now let us get her into it. That's capitally done. Put the baby inside as well; it will hold them both comfortably. Button it over them. There, that will keep them nice and warm. Do you know her? Does she live far from here? Is she the woman you are looking for?"

"Yes, and her lodging is a mile away. How can we get her home?"

"We'll manage it. Ah, we're in luck. Here's a cab coming towards us. Hold on to them while I speak to the driver."

He was off and back again with the cab—with the driver of which he had made a rapid bargain—in a wonderfully short space of time. The mother and her babe were lifted tenderly in, the address was given to the driver, the two kind-hearted men took their seats, the windows were pulled up, and the cab crawled slowly on towards Mrs. Turner's lodging. Dr. Spenlove's skilful hands were busy over the woman, restoring animation to her frozen limbs, and Mr. Moss was doing the same to the child.

"How are you getting along, doctor? I am progressing famously, famously. The child is warming up, and is beginning to breathe quite nicely."

He was handling the babe as tenderly as if it were a child of his own.

"She will recover, I trust," said Dr. Spenlove; "but we were only just in time. It is fortunate that I met you, Mr. Moss; you have been the means of saving two helpless, unfortunate beings."

"Nonsense, nonsense," answered Mr. Moss. "I have only done what any man would do. It is you who have saved them, doctor, not I. I am proud to know you, and I shall be glad to hear of your getting along in the world. You haven't done very well up to now, I fear. Go for the big fish and the big birds, doctor."

"If that were the universal law of life," asked Dr. Spenlove, in a tone of exquisite compassion, with a motion of his hands towards Mrs. Turner and her child, "what would become of these?"

"Ah, yes, yes," responded Mr. Moss, gravely; "but I mean in a general way, you know. To be sure, there are millions more little fish and birds than there are big ones, but it's a selfish world, doctor."

"You are not an exemplification of it," said Dr. Spenlove, his eyes brightening. "The milk of human kindness will never be frozen, even on such bitter nights as this, while men like you are in it."

"You make me ashamed of myself," cried Mr. Moss, violently, but instantly sobered down. "And now, as I see we are close to the poor woman's house, perhaps you will tell me what more I can do."

Dr. Spenlove took from his pocket the money with which he had intended to pay his fare to London, and held it out to Mr. Moss. "Pay the cabman for me, and assist me to carry the woman up to her room."

Mr. Moss thrust the money back. "I will pay him myself; it is my cab, not yours. I don't allow any one to get the better of me if I can help it."

When the cab stopped he jumped out and settled with the driver, and then he and Dr. Spenlove carried Mrs. Turner and her babe to the top of the house. The room was dark and cold, and Mr. Moss shivered. He struck a match, and held it while Dr. Spenlove laid the mother and child upon their wretched bed.

"Kindly stop here a moment," said the doctor.

He went into the passage, and called to the lodger on the same floor of whom he had made inquiries earlier in the night. She soon appeared, and after they had exchanged a few words, accompanied him, but partially dressed, to Mrs. Turner's room. She brought a lighted candle with her, and upon Mr. Moss taking it from her, devoted herself, with Dr. Spenlove, to her fellow-lodger and the babe.

"Dear, dear, dear!" she said, piteously. "Poor soul, poor soul!"

Mr. Moss was not idle. All the finer qualities of his nature were stirred to action by the adventures of the night. He knelt before the grate; it was empty; not a cinder had been left; some grey ashes on the hearth—that was all. He looked into the broken coal scuttle; it had been scraped bare. Rising to his feet he stepped to the cupboard; a cracked cup and saucer were there, a chipped plate or two, a mouthless jug, but not a vestige of food. Without a word he left the room, and sped downstairs.

He was absent fifteen or twenty minutes, and when he returned it was in the company of a man who carried a hundredweight of coals upon his shoulders. Mr. Moss himself was loaded : under his armpits two bundles of wood and a loaf of bread ; in one hand tea and butter ; in his other hand a can of milk.

"God bless you, sir!" said the woman, who was assisting Dr. Spenlove.

Mr. Moss knelt again before the grate, and made a fire. Kettle in hand he searched for water.

"You will find some in my room, sir," said the woman.

Mrs. Turner and her babe were now in bed, the child still craving for food, the mother still unconscious, but breathing heavily. The fire lit, and the kettle on, Mr. Moss put on his fur overcoat, whispered a good-night to Dr. Spenlove, received a grateful pressure of the hand in reply, slipped out of the house, and took his way home, humming—

> "O del ciel angeli immortal,
> Deh mi guidate con voi lassù!
> Dio giusto, a te m'abbandono,
> Buon Dio m'accorda il tuo perdono!"

He looked at his hands, which were black from contact with the coals.

"What will Mrs. Moss say?" he murmured.

CHAPTER VII.

AN hour after Mr. Moss's departure Mrs. Turner opened her eyes. It was a moment for which Dr. Spenlove had anxiously waited. He had satisfied himself that both of his patients were in a fair way of recovery, and thus far his heart was relieved. The woman who had assisted him had also taken her departure after having given the babe some warm milk. Her hunger appeased, the little one was sleeping calmly and peacefully by her mother's side.

The room was now warm and cheerful. A bright fire was blazing, the kettle was simmering, and a pot of hot tea was standing on the hearth.

Mrs. Turner gazed around in bewilderment. The one candle in the room but dimly lighted it up, and the flickering flames of the fire threw fantastic shadows on walls and ceiling ; but so bright was the blaze that there was nothing distressful in these

72

shadowy phantasmagoria. At a little distance from the bed stood Dr. Spenlove, his pale face turned to the waking woman. She looked at him long and steadily, and did not answer him when he smiled encouragingly at her and spoke a few gentle words. She passed her hand over the form of her sleeping child, and then across her forehead, in the effort to recall what had passed. But her mind was confused ; bewildering images of the stages of her desperate resolve presented themselves—blinding snow, shrieking wind, the sea which she had not reached, the phantoms she had conjured up when her senses were deserting her in the white streets.

"Am I alive?" she muttered.

"Happily, dear Mrs. Turner," said Dr. Spenlove. "You are in your own room, and you will soon be well."

"Who brought me here?"

"I, and a good friend I was fortunate enough to meet when I was seeking you."

"Why did you seek me?"

"To save you."

"To save me! You knew, then—— "

She paused.

"I knew nothing except that you were in trouble."

" Where did you find me ? "

" In the snow, you and your child. A few minutes longer, and it would have been too late. But an angel directed my steps."

" No angel directed you : a devil led you on. Why did you not leave me to die? It was what I went out for. I confess it ! " she cried, recklessly. " It was my purpose not to live ; it was my purpose not to allow my child to live ! I was justified. Is not a quick death better than a slow, lingering torture which must end in death ? Why did you save me? Why did you not leave me to die ? "

" It would have been a crime."

" It would have been a mercy. You have brought me back to misery. I do not thank you, doctor."

" You may live to thank me. Drink this tea ; it will do you good."

She shook her head rebelliously.

" What is the use ? You have done me an ill turn. Had it not been for you I should have been at peace. There would have been no more hunger, no more privation. There would have been an end to my shame and degradation."

" You would have taken it with you to the Judgment Seat," said Dr. Spenlove, with solemn tenderness.

"There would have been worse than hunger and privation. What answer could you have made to the Eternal when you presented yourself before the Throne with the crime of murder on your soul?"

"Murder!" she gasped.

"Murder," he gently repeated. "If you went out to-night with an intention so appalling, it was not only your own life you would have taken, it was the life of the innocent babe now slumbering by your side. Can you have forgotten that?"

"No," she answered, in a tone of faint defiance, "I have not forgotten it, I do not forget it. God would have forgiven me."

"He would not have forgiven you."

"He would. What has she to live for? What have I to live for—a lost and abandoned woman, a mother whose association would bring degradation upon her child? How should I meet her reproaches when she grew to be a woman herself? I am not ungrateful for what you have done for me"—she glanced at the fire and the tea he held in his hand—"but it cannot continue. To-morrow will come. There is always a to-morrow to strike terror to the hearts of such as I. Do you know what I have suffered? Do you see the future that lies before us?

What hope is there in this world for me and my child?"

"There is hope. You brought her into the world."

"God help me, I did!" she moaned.

"By what right, having given her life, would you rob her of the happiness which may be in store for her?"

"Happiness!" she exclaimed, bitterly. "You speak to me of happiness!"

"I do, in truth and sincerity, if you are willing to make a sacrifice, if you are willing to perform a duty."

"What would I not be willing to do," she cried, despairingly; "what would I not cheerfully do, to make her life innocent and happy—not like mine— oh, not like mine! But you are mocking me with empty words."

"Indeed I am not," said Dr. Spenlove, earnestly. "Since I left you some hours ago, not expecting to see you again, something has occurred of which I came to speak to you. I found your room deserted, and feared—what we will not mention again. I searched, and discovered you in time to save you; and with all my heart I thank God for it! Now, drink this tea. I have much to say to you, and you need strength to consider it. If you can eat a little bread and butter—ah, you can! Let me fill your cup again. That is right. Now I recognise the lady it was my pleasure to be able to assist, not to the extent I would have wished, because of my own circumstances."

His reference to her as a lady, no less than the respectful consideration of his manner towards her, brought a flush to her cheeks as she ate. And, indeed, she ate ravenously. Defiant and rebellious as may be our moods, nature's demands are imperative, and no mortal is strong enough to resist them.

When she had finished he sat by her side, and was silent awhile, debating with himself how he should approach the task which Mr. Gordon had imposed upon him.

She saved him the trouble of commencing.

" Are you acquainted with the story of my life ? " she asked.

" It has been imparted to me," he replied, " by one to whom I was a stranger till within the last few hours."

" Do I know him ? "

" You know him well."

For a moment she thought of the man who had

brought her to this gulf of shame, but she dismissed the thought. It was impossible. He was too heartless and base to send a messenger to her on an errand of friendship, and Dr. Spenlove would have undertaken no errand of an opposite nature.

" Will you tell me his name ? "

" Mr. Gordon."

She trembled, and her face grew white. She had wronged this man ; the law might say that she had robbed him. Oh ! why had her fatal design been frustrated ? why was not this torturing existence ended ?

" You need be under no apprehension," continued Dr. Spenlove ; " he comes as a friend."

She tossed her head in scorn of herself as one unworthy of friendship.

" He has but lately arrived in England from the Colonies, and he came with the hope of taking you back with him as his wife. It is from him I learned the sad particulars of your life. Believe me when I say that he is desirous to befriend you."

" In what way ? Does he offer me money ? I have cost him enough already. My father tricked him, and I have shamefully deceived him. To receive more from him would fill me with shame ; but for the sake of my child I will submit to any sacrifice, to any humiliation—I will do anything, anything! It would well become me to show pride when charity is offered to me!"

"Do not forget those words—'for the sake of your child you will submit to any sacrifice.' It is your duty, for her sake, to accept any honourable proposition, and Mr. Gordon offers nothing that is not honourable." (He sighed as he said this, for he thought of the sacredness of a mother's love for her first-born.) "He will not give you money apart from himself. United to him, all he has is yours. He wishes to marry you."

She stared at him in amazement.

"Are you mad!" she cried, "or do you think that I am?".

"I am speaking the sober truth. Mr. Gordon has followed you here because he wishes to marry you."

"Knowing me for what I am!" she said, still incredulous. "Knowing that I am in the lowest depths of degradation; knowing this"—she touched her child with a gentle hand—"he wishes to marry me!"

"He knows all. There is not an incident in your

career with which he does not seem to be acquainted,
and in the errand with which he has charged me he is
sincerely in earnest."

"Dr. Spenlove," she said, slowly, "what is your
opinion of a man who comes forward to pluck from
shame and poverty a woman who has behaved as I
have to Mr. Gordon?"

"His actions speak for him," replied Dr. Spenlove.

"He must have a noble nature," she said. "I
never regarded him in that light. I took him to be
a hard, conscientious, fair-dealing man, who thought
I would make him a good wife, but I never believed
that he loved me. I did him the injustice of supposing him incapable of love. Ah, how I misjudged
this man! I am not worthy of him, I am not worthy
of him!"

"Set your mind not upon the past, but upon the
future. Think of yourself and of your child in the
years to come, and remember the fear and horror by
which you have been oppressed in your contemplation of them. I have something further to disclose
to you. Mr. Gordon imposes a condition from which
he will not swerve, and to which I beg you to listen
with calmness. When you have heard all, do not
answer hastily. Reflect upon the consequences

which hang on your decision, and bear in mind that you have to make that decision before I leave you. I am to bear your answer to him to-night ; he is waiting in my rooms to receive it."

Then, softening down all that was harsh in the proposal and magnifying all its better points, Dr. Spenlove related to her what had passed between Mr. Gordon and himself. She listened in silence, and he could not judge from her demeanour whether he was to succeed or to fail. Frequently she turned her face from his tenderly-searching gaze, as though more effectually to conceal her thoughts from him. When he finished speaking she showed that she had taken to heart his counsel not to decide hastily, for she did not speak for several minutes. Then she said plaintively,—

" There is no appeal, doctor ? "

" None," he answered, in a decisive tone.

" He sought you out and made you his messenger, because of his impression that you had influence with me, and would advise me for my good ? "

" As I have told you, in his own words, as nearly as I have been able to recall them."

" He was right. There is no man in the world I honour more than I honour you. I would accept

what you say against my own convictions, against
my own feelings. Advise me, doctor. My mind is
distracted ; I cannot be guided by it. You know
what I am, you know what I have been, you foresee
the future that lies before me. Advise me."

The moment he had dreaded had arrived. The
issue was with him. He felt that this woman's fate
was in his hands.

" My advice is," he said, in a low tone, " that you
accept Mr. Gordon's offer."

" And cast aside a mother's duty ? "

" What did you cast aside," he asked, sadly, " when
you went with your child on such a night as this
towa ds the sea ? "

She shuddered. She would not look at her child ;
with stern resolution she kept her eyes from wandering to the spot upon which the infant lay ; she even
moved away from the little body so that she should
not come in contact with it.

A long silence ensued, which Dr. Spenlove dared
not break.

" I cannot blame him," she then said, her voice,
now and again, broken by a sob, " for making conditions. It is his respectability that is at stake, and
he is noble and generous for taking such a risk upon

himself. There is a law for the man and a law for
the woman. Oh, I know what I am saying, doctor ;
the lesson has been driven into my soul, and I have
learnt it with tears of blood. One of these laws is
white, the other black, and justice says it is right.
It is our misfortune that we bear the children, and
that their little fingers clutch our heart-strings. It
would be mockery for me to say that I love my child
with a love equal to that I should have felt if she had
come into the world without the mark of shame with
which I have branded her. With my love for her is
mingled a loathing of myself, a terror of the living
evidence of my fall. But I love her, doctor, I love
her—and never yet so much as now when I am asked
to part with her! What I did a while ago was done
in a frenzy of despair. I had no food, you see, and
she was crying for it ; and the horror and the anguish
of that hour may overpower me again if I am left as
I am. I will accept Mr. Gordon's offer, and I will
be as good a wife to him as it is in my power to be ;
but I, also, have a condition to make. Mr. Gordon is
much older than I, and it may be that I shall outlive
him. The condition I make is—and whatever the
consequences I am determined to abide by it—that in
the event of my husband's death, and of there being

no children of our union, I shall be free to seek the child I am called upon to desert. In everything else I will perform my part of the contract faithfully. Take my decision to Mr. Gordon, and if it is possible for you to return here to-night with his answer, I implore you to do so. I cannot close my eyes, I cannot rest, until I hear the worst. God alone knows on which side lies the right, on which the wrong ! "

" I will return with his answer," said Dr. Spenlove, " to-night."

" There is still something more," she said, in an imploring tone, "and it must be a secret sacredly kept between you and me. It may happen that you will become acquainted with the name of the guardian of my child. I have a small memorial which I desire he shall retain until she is of age, say until she is twenty-one, or until, in the event of my husband's death, I am free to seek her in years to come. If you do not discover who the guardian is, I ask you to keep this memorial for me until I reclaim it ; which may be, never ! Will you do this for me ? "

" I will."

" Thank you for all your goodness to me. But I have nothing to put the memorial in. Could you add to your many kindnesses by giving me a small box which I can lock and secure? Dear Dr. Spenlove, it is a mother who will presently be torn from her child who implores you!"

He bethought him of a small iron box he had at home, which contained some private papers of his own. He could spare this box without inconvenience to himself, and he promised to bring it to her; and so, with sincere words of consolation, he left her.

In the course of an hour he returned. Mr. Gordon had consented to the condition she imposed.

"Should I be thankful or not?" she asked, wistfully.

"You should be thankful," he replied. "Your child, rest assured, will have a comfortable and happy home. Here is the box and the key. It is a patent lock; no other key can open it. I will show you how to use it. Yes, that is the way." He paused a moment, his hand in his pocket. "You will be ready to meet Mr. Gordon at two to-morrow?"

"And my child?" she asked, with tears in her voice. "When will she be taken from me?"

"At twelve." His hand was still fumbling in his pocket, and he suddenly shook his head, as if indignant with himself. "You may want to purchase one or two little things in the morning. Here are a few shillings. Pray accept them."

He laid on the table the money with which he had intended to pay his fare to London.

"Heaven reward you," said the grateful woman, "and make your life bright and prosperous."

Her tears bedewed his hand as she kissed it humbly, and Dr. Spenlove walked wearily home, once more penniless, but not entirely unhappy.

CHAPTER VIII.

THE mother's vigil with her child on this last night was fraught with conflicting emotions of agony and rebellion. Upon Dr. Spenlove's departure she rose and dressed herself completely, all her thoughts and feelings being so engrossed by the impending separation that she took no heed of her damp clothes. She entertained no doubt that the renunciation was imperative and in the interest of her babe ; nor did she doubt that the man who had dictated it was acting in simple justice to himself and in a spirit of mercy towards her ; but she was in no mood to regard with gratitude one who in the most dread crisis in her life had saved her from destruction. The cause of this injustice lay in the fact that until this moment the true maternal instinct had not been awakened within her breast. As she had faithfully expressed it to Dr. Spenlove, the birth of her babe had filled her

with terror and with a loathing of herself. Had
there been no consequences of her error apparent
to the world she would have struggled on and might
have been able to preserve her good name ; her
dishonour would not have been made clear to
censorious eyes ; but the living evidence of her
shame was by her side, and, left to her own resources,
she had conceived the idea that death was her
only refuge. Her acceptance of the better course
that had been opened for her loosened the flood-
gates of tenderness for the child who was soon to
be torn from her arms. Love and remorse shone
in her eyes as she knelt by the bedside and fondled
the little hands and kissed the innocent lips.

"Will you not wake, darling," she murmured,
"and let me see your dear eyes? Wake, darling,
wake! Do you not know what is going to happen?
They are going to take you from me. Perhaps we
shall never meet again ; and if we do, you have
not even a name by which I can call you. But
perhaps that will not matter. Surely you will know
your mother, surely I shall know my child, and
we shall fly to each other's arms. I want to tell you
all this—I want you to hear it. Wake, sweet,
wake ! "

The child slept on. Presently she murmured, " It is hard, it is hard ! How can God permit such cruelty ? "

Half an hour passed in this way, and then she became more composed. Her mind, which had been unbalanced by her misfortunes, recovered its equilibrium, and she could reason with comparative calmness upon the future. In sorrow and pain she mentally mapped out the years to come. She saw her future, as she believed, a joyless life, a life of cold duty. She would not entertain the possibility of a brighter side, the possibility of her becoming reconciled to her fate, of her growing to love her husband, of her having other children who would be as dear to her as this one was. In the state of her feelings it seemed to her monstrous to entertain such ideas, a wrong perpetrated upon the babe she was deserting. In dogged rebellion she hugged misery to her breast, and dwelt upon it as part of the punishment she had brought upon herself. There was no hope of happiness for her in the future, there was no ray of light to illumine her path. For ever would she be thinking of the child for whom now, for the first time since its birth, she felt a mother's love, and who was henceforth to find a home among strangers.

In this hopeless fashion did she muse for some time, and then a star appeared in her dark sky. She might, as she had suggested to Dr. Spenlove, survive her husband; it was more than possible, it was probable, and, though there was in the contemplation a touch of treason towards the man who had come to her rescue, she derived satisfaction from it. In the event of his death she must adopt some steps to prove that the child was hers, and that she, and she alone, had the sole right to her. No stranger should keep her darling from her, should rob her of her reward for the sufferings she had undergone. It was for this reason that she had asked Dr. Spenlove for the iron box.

It was a compact, well-made box, and very heavy for its size. Any person receiving it as a precious deposit, under the conditions she imposed, might, when it was in his possession, reasonably believe that it contained mementoes of price, valuable jewels, perhaps, which she wished her child to wear when she grew to womanhood. She had no such treasure. Unlocking the box she took from her pocket a packet of letters, which she read with a bitterness which displayed itself strongly in her face, which made her quiver with passionate indignation.

" The villain ! " she muttered. " If he stood before me now, I would strike him dead at my feet."

There was no lingering accent of tenderness in her voice. The love she had for him but yesterday was dead, and for the father of her child she had now only feelings of hatred and scorn. Clearly she was a woman of strong passions, a woman who could love and hate with ardour.

The letters were four in number, and had been written, at intervals of two or three weeks, by the man who had betrayed and deserted her. The language was such as would have deceived any girl who had given him her heart. The false fervour, the, protestations of undying love, the passionate appeals to put full trust in his honour, were sufficient to stamp the writer as a heartless villain, and, if he aped respectability, to ruin him in the eyes of the world. Cunning he must have been to a certain extent, but it was evident that, in thus incriminating himself and supplying proofs of his perfidy, he had forgotten his usual caution. Perhaps he had been for a short time under a delusion that in his pursuit of the girl he was acting honourably and sincerely, or perhaps (which is more likely), finding that she held back, he was so eager to win her that he addressed her in the only way by which he could compass his desire. The last of the four letters contained a solemn promise of marriage if she would leave her home, and place herself under his protection. It even went so far as to state that he had the license ready, and that it was only her presence that was needed to ratify their union. There was a reference in this letter to the engagement between her and Mr. Gordon, and the writer declared that it would bring misery upon her. "Release yourself from this man," he continued, "at once and for ever. It would be a living death. Rely upon my love. All my life shall be devoted to the task of making you happy, and you shall never have occasion for one moment's regret that you have consented to be guided by me." She read these words with a smile of bitter contempt on her lips, and a burning desire in her heart for revenge.

"If there is justice in heaven," she muttered, "a day will come!"

Then she brought forward a photograph of the betrayer, which, with the letters, she deposited in the box. This done, she locked the box, and tying the key to a bit of string, hung it round her neck, and allowed it to fall, hidden, in her bosom.

Seating herself by the bedside, she gazed upon the babe from whom she was soon to be torn. Her eyes were filled with tears, and her sad thoughts, shaped in words, ran somewhat in this fashion :

"In a few hours she will be taken from me ; in a few short hours we shall be separated, and then, and then—ah, how can I know it and live!—an ocean of waters will divide us. She will not miss me ; she does not know me. She will receive another woman's endearments ; she will never bestow a thought upon me, her wretched mother, and I—I shall be for ever thinking of her! She is all my own now ; presently I shall have no claim upon her. Would it not be better to end it as I had intended—to end it now, this moment!" She rose to her feet, and stood with her lips tightly pressed and her hands convulsively clenched ; and then she cried in horror, "No, no! I dare not—I dare not! It would be murder, and he said that God would not forgive me. Oh, my darling, my darling, it is merciful that you are a baby, and do not know what is passing in my mind! If you do not love me now, you may in the future, when I shall

be free, and then you shall feel how different is a
mother's love from the love of a strange woman.
But how shall I recognise you if you are a woman
before we meet again—how shall I prove to you,
to the world, that you are truly mine? Your eyes
will be black, as mine are, and your hair, I hope,
will be as dark, but there are thousands like that.
I am grateful that you resemble me, and not your
base father, whom I pray God to strike and punish.
Oh, that it were ever in my power to repay him
for his treachery, to say to him, ' As you dragged
me down, so do I drag you down ! As you ruined
my life, so do I ruin yours !' But I cannot hope
for that. The woman weeps, the man laughs. Never
mind, child, never mind. If in future years we
are reunited, it will be happiness enough. Dark
hair, black eyes, small hands and feet. Oh, darling,
darling!" She covered the little hands and feet
with kisses. "And yes, yes"—with feverish eager-
ness she gazed at the child's neck—"these two tiny
moles, like those on my neck. I shall know you,
I shall know you, I shall be able to prove that you
are my daughter ! "

With a lighter heart she resumed her seat, and
set to work mending the infant's scanty clothing,

which she fondled and kissed as though it had sense and feeling. A church clock in the distance tolled five. She had been listening for the hour, hoping it was earlier.

" Five o'clock ! " she muttered. " I thought it was not later than three. I am being robbed. Oh, if time would only stand still! Five o'clock! In seven hours she will be taken from me. Seven hours—seven short hours ! I will not close my eyes."

But after awhile her lids drooped, and she was not conscious of it. The abnormal fatigues of the day and night, the relaxing of the overstrung nerves, the warmth of the room, produced their effect; her head sank upon the bed, and she fell into a dreamful sleep.

It was merciful that her dreaming fancies were not drawn from the past. The psychological cause of her slumbers being beguiled by bright visions may be found in the circumstance that, despite the conflicting passions by which she had been agitated, the worldly ease which was secured to her and her child by Mr. Gordon's offer had re-moved a heavy weight from her heart. In her visions she saw her baby grow into a happy girlhood ; she had glimpses of holiday times, when they were together in the fields or by the seaside, or walking in the glow of lovely sunsets, gathering flowers in the hush of the woods, or winding their way through the golden corn. In these fair dreams her baby passed from girlhood to womanhood, and happy smiles wreathed the lips of the woe-worn woman as she lay in her poor garments on the humble bed by the side of her child.

"Do you love me, darling?" asked the sleeping mother.

"Dearly, dearly," answered the dream-child. "With my whole heart, mother."

"Call me mother again. It is like the music of the angels."

"Mother, mother!"

"You will love me always, darling?"

"Always, mother ; for ever and ever and ever."

"Say that you will never love me less, that you will never forget me."

"I will never love you less ; I will never forget you."

"Darling child, how beautiful you are! There is not in the world a lovelier woman. It is for me to protect and guard you. I can do so: I have had experience. Come, let us rest."

They sat upon a mossy bank, and the mother folded her arms around her child, who lay slumbering on her breast.

There had been a few blissful days in this woman's life, during which she had believed in man's faithfulness and God's goodness, but the dreaming hours she was now enjoying were fraught with a heavenly gladness. Nature and dreams are the fairies of the poor and the afflicted.

She awoke as the church clock chimed eight. Again had she to face the stern realities of life. The sad moment of separation was fast approaching.

CHAPTER IX.

AT five o'clock on the afternoon of that day Dr.
Spenlove returned to his apartments. Having given
away the money with which he had intended to
pay his fare to London, he had bethought him of
a gentleman living in Southsea of whom he thought
he could borrow a sovereign or two for a few weeks.
He had walked the distance, and had met with disappointment ; the gentleman was absent on business,
and might be absent several days.

"Upon my word," said the good doctor, as he
drearily retraced his steps, "it is almost as bad as
being shipwrecked ; worse, because there are no
railways on desert islands. What on earth am I
to do ? Get to London I must, by hook or by crook,
and there is absolutely nothing I can turn into money."

Then he bethought himself of Mr. Moss, and in
his extremity determined to make an appeal in that
quarter. Had it not been for what had occurred

last night, he would not have dreamed of going to this gentleman, of whose goodness of heart he had had no previous experience, and upon whose kindness he had not the slightest claim. Arriving at Mr. Moss's establishment, another disappointment attended him. Mr. Moss was not at home, and they could not say when he would return. So Dr. Spenlove, greatly depressed, walked slowly on, his mind distressed with troubles and perplexities.

He had seen nothing more of Mr. Gordon, who had left him in the early morning with a simple acknowledgment in words of the service he had rendered ; nor had he seen anything further of Mrs. Turner. On his road home he called at her lodgings, and heard from her fellow-lodger that she had left the house.

" We don't know where she's gone to, sir," the woman said ; " but the rent has been paid up, and a sovereign was slipped under my door. If it wasn't that she was so hard up I should have thought it came from her."

" I have no doubt it did," Dr. Spenlove answered. " She has friends who are well-to-do, and I know that one of these friends, discovering her position, was anxious to assist her."

"I am glad to hear it," said the woman; "and it was more than kind of her to remember me. I always had an idea that she was above us."

As he was entering his room his landlady ran up from the kitchen.

"Oh, doctor, there's a parcel and two letters for you in your room, and Mr. Moss has been here to see you. He said he would come again."

"Very well, Mrs. Radcliffe," said Dr. Spenlove; and, cheered by the news of the promised visit, he passed into his apartment. On the table were the letters and the parcel. The latter, carefully wrapped in thick brown paper, was the iron box he had given to Mrs. Turner. One of the letters was in her handwriting, and it informed him that her child had been taken away and that she was on the point of leaving Portsmouth.

"I am not permitted," the letter ran, "to inform you where I am going, and I am under the obligation of not writing to you personally after I leave this place. This letter is sent without the knowledge of the gentleman for whom you acted, and I do not consider myself bound to tell him that I have written it. What I have promised to do I will do faithfully, but nothing further. You, who of all

men in the world perhaps know me best, will understand what I am suffering as I pen these lines. I
send with my letter the box you were kind enough
to give me last night. It contains the memorial
of which I spoke to you. Dear Dr. Spenlove, I
rely upon you to carry out my wishes with respect
to it. If you are acquainted with the guardian of
my child, convey it to him, and beg him to retain
it until my darling is of age, or until I am free
to seek her. It is not in your nature to refuse the
petition of a heartbroken mother; it is not in your
nature to violate a promise. For all the kindnesses
you have shown me receive my grateful and
humble thanks. That you will be happy and
successful, and that God will prosper you in all
your undertakings, will be my constant prayer.
Farewell."

Laying this letter aside he opened the second,
which was in a handwriting strange to him :—

" DEAR SIR,—

" All my arrangements are made, and the
business upon which we spoke together is satisfactorily
concluded. You will find enclosed a practical expression of my thanks. I do not give you my

address for two reasons. First, I desire no acknowledgment of the enclosure ; second, I desire that
there shall be no correspondence between us upon
any subject. Feeling perfectly satisfied that the
confidence I reposed in you will be respected,

"I am,

"Your obedient servant,

"G. GORDON."

The enclosure consisted of five Bank of England
notes for £20 each.

Dr. Spenlove was very much astonished and very
much relieved. At this juncture the money was a
fortune to him ; there was a likelihood of its proving
the turning-point in his career ; and, although it had
not been earned in the exercise of his profession, he
had no scruple in accepting it. The generosity of
the donor was, moreover, in some sense an assurance
that he was sincere in all the professions he had made.

"Mr. Moss, sir," said Mrs. Radcliffe, opening the
door, and that gentleman entered the room.

As usual, he was humming an operatic air ; but he
ceased as he closed the door, which, after a momentary
pause, he reopened, to convince himself that the landlady was not listening in the passage.

"Can't be too careful, doctor," he observed, with a wink, "when you have something you want to keep to yourself. You have been running after me, and I have been running after you. Did you wish to see me particularly?"

"To tell you the truth," replied Dr. Spenlove, "I had a special reason for calling upon you; but," he added, with a smile, "as it no longer exists, I need not trouble you."

"No trouble, no trouble at all. I am at your service, doctor. Anything I could have done, or can do now, to oblige, you may safely reckon upon. Within limits, you know, within limits."

"Of course; but the necessity is obviated. I intended to ask you to lend me a small sum of money—without security, Mr. Moss."

"I guessed as much. You should have had it, doctor, and no inquiries made, though it isn't the way I usually conduct my business; but there are men you can trust and are inclined to trust, and there are men you wouldn't trust without binding them down hard and fast. Now, if you still need the money, don't be afraid to ask."

"I should not be afraid, but I am in funds. I am not the less indebted to you, Mr. Moss."

"All right; I am glad you don't want a loan. Now for another affair—*my* affair, I suppose I must call it till I have shifted it to other shoulders, which will soon be done."

He paused a moment.

"Dr. Spenlove, that was a strange adventure last night."

"It was; a strange and sad adventure. You behaved very kindly, and I should like to repay what you expended on behalf of the poor lady."

"No, no, doctor; let it rest where it is. I don't acknowledge your right to repay what you don't owe, and perhaps I am none the worse off for what I did. Throw your bread on the waters, you know. My present visit has reference to the lady—as you call her one, I will do the same—we picked out of the snow last night. Did you ever notice that things go in runs?"

"I don't quite follow you."

"A run of rainy weather, a run of fine weather, a run of good fortune, a run of ill fortune."

"Yes, I have observed it."

"You meet a person to-day you have never seen or heard of before. The odds are that you will meet that person to-morrow, and probably the next day as well. You begin to have bad cards, you go on having bad cards ; you begin to make money, you go on making money."

"You infer that there are seasons of circumstances, as of weather. No doubt you are right."

" I know I am right. Making the acquaintance of your friend, Mrs. Turner, last night, in a very extraordinary manner, I am not at all surprised that I have business in hand in which she is concerned. You look astonished ; but it is true. You gave her a good character, doctor."

" Which she deserves. It happens in life to the best of us that we find ourselves unexpectedly in trouble. Misfortune is a visitor that does not knock at the door ; it enters unannounced."

" We have unlocked the door ourselves, perhaps," suggested Mr. Moss, sagely.

" Quite likely, but we have done so in a moment of trustfulness, deceived by specious professions. The weak and confiding become the victims."

" It is the way of the world, doctor. Hawks and pigeons, you know."

" There are some who are neither," said Dr. Spenlove, who was not disposed to hurry his visitor.

His mind was easy as to his departure from Portsmouth, and he divined from the course the conversation was taking that Mr. Moss had news of a special nature to communicate. He deemed it wisest to allow him to break it in his own way.

"They are the best off," responded Mr. Moss; "brains well balanced—an even scale, doctor—then you can steer straight and to your own advantage. Women are the weakest, as you say ; too much heart, too much sentiment. All very well in its proper place, but it weighs one side of the scale down. Mrs. Moss isn't much better than other women in that respect. She has her whims and crotchets, and doesn't always take the business view."

"Implying that you do, Mr. Moss ? "

"Of course I do ; should be ashamed of myself if I didn't. What do I live for ? Business. What do I live by ? Business. What do I enjoy most? Business, and plenty of it ! "

He rubbed his hands together joyously.

"I should have no objection to paint on my shop door, ' Mr. Moss, Business Man.' People would know it would be no use trying to get the best of me. They don't get it as it is."

"You are unjust to yourself. Was it business last night that made you pay the cabman, and sent you out to buy coals and food for an unfortunate creature you had never seen before ? "

"That was 'a little luxury," said Mr. Moss, with a sly chuckle, "which we business men indulge in occasionally to sharpen up our faculties. It is an investment, and it pays ; it puts us on good terms with ourselves. If you think I have a bit of sentiment in me you are mistaken."

"I paint your portrait for myself," protested Dr. Spenlove, "and I shall not allow you to dis-figure it. Granted that you keep as a rule to the main road—Business Road, we will call it, if you like—— "

"Very good, doctor, very good."

"You walk along, driving bargains, and making money honestly—— "

"Thank you, doctor," interposed Mr. Moss, rather gravely. "There are people who don't do us so much justice."

"When unexpectedly," continued Dr. Spenlove, with tender gaiety, "you chance upon a little narrow path to the right or the left of you, and, your eye lighting on it, you observe a stretch of woodland, a touch of bright colour, a picture of human suffering, that appeals to your poetical instinct, to your musical

tastes, or to your humanity. Down you plunge towards it, to the confusion, for the time being, of
Business Road and its business attractions."

"Sir," said Mr. Moss, bending his head with a
dignity which did not sit ill on him, "if all men were
of your mind the narrow prejudices of creed would
stand a bad chance of making themselves felt. But
we are wandering from the main road of the purpose
which brought me here. I have not said a word to
Mrs. Moss of the adventure of last night; I don't
quite know why, because a better creature doesn't
breathe; but I gathered from you in some way that
you would prefer we should keep it to ourselves.
Mrs. Moss never complains of my being out late; she
rather encourages me, and that will give you an idea
of the good wife she is. 'Enjoyed yourself, Moss?'
she asked when I got home. 'Very much,' I answered,
and that was all. Now, doctor, a business man
wouldn't be worth his salt if he wasn't a thinking
man as well. After I was dressed this morning I
thought a good deal of the lady and her child, and
I came to the conclusion that you took more than
an ordinary interest in them."

"You were right," said Dr. Spenlove.

"Following your lead, which is a good thing to do

if you've confidence in your partner, I found myself taking more than an ordinary interest in them ; but as it wasn't a game of whist we were playing, I had no clue to the cards you held. You will see presently what I am leading up to. While I was thinking and going over some stock which I am compelled by law to put up to auction, I received a message that a gentleman wished to see me on very particular private business. It was then about half-past nine, and the gentleman remained with me about an hour. When he went away he made an appointment with me to meet him at a certain place at twelve o'clock. I met him there ; he had a carriage waiting. I got in, and where do you think he drove me ? "

" I would rather you answered the question yourself," said Dr. Spenlove, his interest in the conversation receiving an exciting stimulus.

" The carriage, doctor, stopped at the house to which we conveyed your lady friend and her child last night. I opened my eyes, I can tell you. Now, not to beat about the bush, I will make you acquainted with the precise nature of the business the gentleman had with me."

" Pardon me a moment," said Dr. Spenlove. " Was Mr. Gordon the gentleman ? "

"You have named him," said Mr. Moss, and per-
ceiving that Dr. Spenlove was about to speak again,
he contented himself with answering the question.
But the doctor did not proceed ; his first intention
had been to inquire whether the business was con-
fidential, and if so to decline to listen to the disclosure
which his visitor desired to make. A little consideration, however, inclined him to the opinion that this
might be carrying delicacy too far. He was in the
confidence of both Mr. Gordon and Mrs. Turner,
and it might be prejudicial to the mother and her
child if he closed his ears to the issue of the strange
adventure. He waved his hand, thereby inviting
Mr. Moss to continue.

"Just so, doctor," said Mr. Moss, in the tone of a
man who had disposed of an objection. "It is a
singular business, but I have been mixed up with
all kinds of queer transactions in my time, and I
always give a man the length of his rope. What
induced Mr. Gordon to apply to me is his concern,
not mine. Perhaps he had heard a good report of
me, and I am much obliged to those who gave it ;
perhaps he thought I was a tradesman who would
take anything in pledge, from a flat iron to a flesh
and blood baby. Any way, if I choose to regard his

visit as a compliment, it is because I am not thin-skinned. Mr. Gordon informed me that he wished to find a home and to provide for a young baby whose mother could not look after it, being im-peratively called away to a distant part of the world. Had it not been that the terms he proposed were extraordinarily liberal, and that he gave me the names of an eminent firm of lawyers in London who had undertaken the financial part of the business, and had it not been, also, that as he spoke to me I thought of a friend whom it might be in my power to serve, I should have shut him up at once by saying that I was not a baby farmer, and by request-ing him to take his leave. Interrupting myself, and as it was you who first mentioned the name of Mr. Gordon, I think I am entitled to ask if you are acquainted with him ? "

" You are entitled to ask the question. I am acquainted with him."

" Since when, doctor ? "

" Since last night only."

" Before we met ? "

" Yes, before we met."

" May I inquire if you were then acting for Mr. Gordon ? "

"To some extent. Had it not been for him I
should not have gone in search of Mrs. Turner."

"In which case," said Mr. Moss, in a grave tone,
"she and her child would have been found dead in
the snow. That is coming to first causes, doctor. I
have not been setting a trap for you in putting these
questions ; I have been testing Mr. Gordon's veracity.
When I asked him whether I was the only person in
Portsmouth whom he had ·consulted, he frankly
answered I was not. Upon this I insisted upon his
telling me who this other person was. After some
hesitation he said, ' Dr. Spenlove.' Any scruples I
may have had were instantly dispelled, for I knew
that it was impossible you could be mixed up in a
business which had not a good end."

"I thank you."

"Hearing your name I thought at once of the lady
and her child whom we were instrumental in saving.
Am I right in my impression that you are in
possession of the conditions and terms Mr. Gordon
imposes ? "

"I am."

"Then I need not go into them. I take it, Dr.
Spenlove, that you do not consider the business
disreputable."

"It is not disreputable. Mr. Gordon is a peculiar man, and his story in connection with the lady in question is a singular one. He is not the father of the child, and the action he has taken is not prompted by a desire to rid himself of a responsibility. On the contrary, out of regard for the lady he has voluntarily incurred a very heavy responsibility, which I have little doubt—none, indeed—that he will honourably discharge."

"I will continue. Having heard what Mr. Gordon had to say—thinking all the time of the friend who might be induced to adopt the child, and that I might be able to serve him—I put the gentleman to the test. Admitting that his terms were liberal, I said that a sum of money ought to be paid down at once, in proof of his good faith. 'How much?' he asked. 'Fifty pounds,' I answered. He instantly produced the sum, in bank-notes. Then it occurred to me that it would make things still safer if I had an assurance from the eminent firm of London lawyers that the business was honourable and met with their approval; and if I also had a notification from them that they were prepared to pay the money regularly. 'Send them a telegram,' suggested Mr. Gordon, 'and make it full and complete. I will write a shorter

one, which you can send at the same time. Let the
answers be addressed here, and open them both
yourself when they arrive, which should be before
twelve o'clock.' The telegrams written, I took them
to the office ; and before twelve came the replies,
which were perfectly satisfactory. Everything appeared to be so straightforward that I undertook the
business. A singular feature in it is that Mr. Gordon
does not wish to know with whom the child is placed.
' My lawyers will make inquiries,' he said, ' and they
will be content if the people are respectable.' Dr.
Spenlove, I thought it right that you should be
informed of what I have done ; you have expressed
your approval, and I am satisfied. Don't you run
away with the idea that I have acted philanthropically.
Nothing of the kind, sir ; I have been paid for my
trouble. And now, if you would like to ask any
questions, fire away."

" Were no conditions of secrecy imposed upon you ? "

" Yes ; but I said that I was bound to confide in
one person. He may have thought I meant Mrs.
Moss, but it was you I had in my mind. I promised
that it should go no further, and I do not intend that
it shall. Mrs. Moss will be none the worse for not
being let into the secret."

" Where is the child now ? "

" In the temporary care of a respectable woman, who is providing suitable clothing for it, Mr. Gordon having given me money for the purpose."

" He has not spared his purse. When do you propose taking the child to her new home ? "

" To-night."

" They are good people ? "

" The best in the world. I would trust my own children with them. She cannot help being happy with them."

" Do they live in Portsmouth ? "

" No ; in Gosport. I think this is as much as I have the right to disclose."

" I agree with you. Mr. Moss, you can render me an obligation, and you can do a kindness to the poor child's mother. She has implored me to endeavour to place this small iron box in the care of the guardians of her child, to be retained by them for twenty-one years, or until the mother claims it, which she will be free to do in the event of her husband dying during her lifetime. I do not know what it contains, and I understand that it is to be given up to no other person than the child or her mother. Will you do this for me or for her ? "

"For both of you, doctor," replied Mr. Moss, lifting the box from the table. "It shall be given into their care, as the mother desires. And now I must be off; I have a busy night before me. Do you go to London to-morrow?"

"A train leaves in a couple of hours; I shall travel by that."

"Well, good-night, and good luck to you. If you want to write to me, you know my address."

They parted with cordiality, and each took his separate way, Dr. Spenlove to the City of Unrest, and Mr. Moss to the peaceful town of Gosport, humming as he went, among other snatches from his favourite opera,—

"Dio dell' or del mondo signor,
Sei possente risplendente,
Sei possente resplendente,
Culto hai tu maggior guaggiù.
Non v'ha un uom che non t'incensi
Stan prostati innanzi a te;
Ed i popolied i re;
I bei scudi tu dispensi,
Del la terra il Dio sei tu."

BOOK THE SECOND.

RACHEL.

CHAPTER X.

THE VISION IN THE CHURCHYARD.

SOME twelve months before the occurrence of the events recorded in the preceding chapters, a Jew, bearing the name of Aaron Cohen, had come to reside in the ancient town of Gosport. He was accompanied by his wife, Rachel. They had no family, and their home was a home of love.

They were comparatively young, Aaron being twenty-eight and Rachel twenty-three, and they had been married five years. Hitherto they had lived in London, and the cause of their taking up their residence in Gosport was that Aaron had conceived the idea that he could establish himself there in a good way of business. One child had blessed their union, whom they called Benjamin. There was great rejoicing at his birth, and it would have been

difficult to calculate how many macaroons and
almond and butter cakes, and cups of chocolate
and glasses of anise-seed, were sacrificed upon the
altar of hospitality in the happy father's house for
several days after the birth of his firstborn. "Aaron
Cohen does it in style," said the neighbours; and as
both he and Rachel were held in genuine respect by
all who knew them, the encomium was not mere
empty praise. Seldom even in the locality in which
the Cohens then resided—the East End of London,
where charity and hospitality are proverbial—had
such feasting been seen at the celebration of a
circumcision. "If he lived in Bayswater," said the
company, "he couldn't have treated us better." And
when the father lifted up his voice and said, "Blessed
art Thou, the Eternal, our God, King of the universe,
who hath sanctified us with His commandments,
and commanded us to introduce our sons into the
covenant of our father Abraham," there was more
than usual sincerity in the response, "Even as this
child has now entered this covenant, so may he be
initiated into the covenant of the law, of marriage,
and of good works." Perhaps among those assembled
there were some who could not have translated into
English the Hebrews' prayers they read so glibly;

but this reproach did not apply to Aaron, who was an erudite as well as an orthodox Jew, and understood every word he uttered. On this memorable day the feasting, commenced in the morning, was continued during the whole day. " I wish you joy, Cohen, I wish you joy ; " this was the formula, a hundred and a hundred times repeated to the proud father, who really believed that a prince had been born among Israel ; while the pale-faced mother, pressing her infant tenderly to her breast, and who in her maidenhood had never looked so beautiful as now, received in her bedroom the congratulations of her intimate female friends. The poorest people in the neighbourhood were welcomed ; and if the seed of good wishes could have blossomed into flower, a rose-strewn path of life lay before the child. " He shall be the son of my right hand," said Aaron Cohen ; and Rachel, as she kissed her child's mouth and tasted its sweet breath, believed that Heaven had descended upon earth, and that no mother had ever been blessed as she was blessed. This precious treasure was the crowning of their love, and they laid schemes for baby's youth and manhood before the child was out of long clothes—schemes destined not to be realised. For sixteen months Benjamin

filled the hearts of his parents with ineffable joy,
and then the Angel of Death entered their house
and bore the young soul away. How they mourned
for the dear one who was nevermore on earth to
rejoice them with his beautiful ways need not here
be related ; all parents who have lost their firstborn
will realise the bitterness of their grief. But not for
long was this grief bitter. In the wise and reverent
interpretation of Aaron Cohen, their loss became a
source of consolation to them. " Let us not rebel,"
he said to his wife, " against the inevitable and
Divine will. Give praise unto the Lord, who has
ordained that we shall have a child in heaven waiting
to receive us." Fraught with tenderness and wisdom
were his words, and his counsel instilled comfort into
Rachel's heart. Benjamin was waiting for them, and
would meet them at the gates. Beautiful was the
thought, radiant the hope it raised, never, never to
fade, nay, to grow brighter even to her dying hour.
Their little child, dead and in his grave, brought
them nearer to God. Heaven and earth were linked
by the spirit of their beloved, who had gone before
them : thus was sorrow sweetened and happiness
chastened by faith. Sitting on their low stools
during the days of mourning, they spoke, when they

were alone, of the peace and joy of the eternal life,
and thereby were drawn spiritually closer to each
other. The lesson they learned in the darkened
room was more precious than jewels and gold; it
is a lesson which comes to all, high and low alike,
and rich indeed are they who learn it aright. For
some time thereafter, when the mother opened the
drawer in which her most precious possessions were
kept, and kissed the little shoes her child had worn,
she would murmur amid her tears,—

"My darling is waiting for me, my darling is
waiting for me!"

God send to all sorrowing mothers a comfort so
sweet!

Aaron Cohen had selected a curious spot in
Gosport for his habitation. The windows of the
house he had taken overlooked the quaint, peaceful
churchyard of the market town. So small and
pretty was this resting-place for the dead, that one
might almost have imagined it to be a burial ground
for children's broken toys. The headless wooden
soldiers, the battered dolls, the maimed contents of
cheap Noah's arks, the thousand and one treasures
of childhood might have been interred there, glad
to be at rest after the ruthless mutilations they

had undergone. For really, in the dawning white
light of a frosty morning, when every object for
miles around sharply outlined itself in the clear
air and seemed to have lost its rotund proportions,
it was hard to realise that, in this tiny churchyard,
men and women, whose breasts once throbbed with
the passions and sorrows of life, were crumbling to
that dust to which we must all return. No, no ;
it could be nothing but the last home of plain and
painted shepherds, and bald-headed pets, and lambs
devoid of fleece, and mayhap—a higher flight which
we all hope to take when the time comes for us
to claim our birthright of the grave—of a dead
bullfinch or canary, carried thither on its back,
with its legs sticking heavenwards, and buried with
grown-up solemnity, and very often with all the
genuineness of grief for a mortal bereavement. Have
you not attended such a funeral, and has not your
overcharged heart caused you to sob in your dreams
as you lay in your cot close to mamma's bed ?

But these fantastic fancies will not serve. It
was a real human churchyard, and Rachel Cohen
knew it to be so as she stood looking out upon it
from the window of her bedroom on the first floor.
It was from no feeling of unhappiness that her

sight became dimmed as she gazed upon the tomb-
stones. Shadows of children rose before her, the
pattering of whose little feet was once the sweetest
music that ever fell on parents' ears, the touch of
whose little hands carried with it an influence as
powerful as a heart-stirring prayer ; children with
golden curls, children with laughing eyes, children
with wistful faces ; but there was one, ah ! there
was one that shone as a star amid the shadows, and
that rose up, up, till it was lost in the solemn
clouds, sending therefrom a Divine message down to
the mother's heart, " Mamma, mamma, I am waiting
for thee ! "

Quiet as was everything around her, Rachel
heard the words ; in the midst of the darkness a
heavenly light was shining on her.

She wiped the tears from her eyes, and stole down
to the room in which her husband was sitting.

CHAPTER XI.

IT was the front room of the house, on the ground floor, which Aaron Cohen had converted into a shop. The small parlour windows had been replaced by larger ones, a counter had been put up, behind which were shelves fitted into the walls. These shelves at present were bare, but Aaron Cohen hoped to see them filled. Under the counter were other shelves, as empty as those on the walls.

When Rachel entered her husband was engaged counting out his money, like the king in his counting house. There was a studious expression on his face, which was instantly replaced by one of deep tenderness as he looked up and saw traces of tears in her eyes. He gathered his money together, bank-notes, silver, gold, and coppers, and motioned her into the room at the rear of the shop. This was their living-room ; but a large iron safe in a corner denoted that it was not to be devoted entirely to

domestic affairs.   In another corner was the symbol
of his business, which was to be affixed to the front
of the premises, over the shop door, the familiar
device of three golden balls.

Letting his money fall upon the table, he drew
his wife to his side, and passed his arm around her.

"The house," he said, "is almost in order."

"Yes, Aaron ; there is very little left to do."

"I am also ready for business.   I have the license,
and to-morrow those glittering balls will be put up
and the name painted over the shop window.   They
are rather large for so small a shop, but they will
attract all the more attention."   He gazed at her
anxiously.   "Do you think you will be contented
and happy here?"

"Contented and happy anywhere with you," she
replied, in a tone of the deepest affection.

"In this town especially, Rachel?"

"Yes, in this town especially.   It is so peaceful."

"But," he said, touching her eyes with his fingers,
"these?"

"Not because I am unhappy," she said ; and her
voice was low and sweet.   "I was looking out upon
the churchyard from our bedroom window."

"Ah!" he said, and he kissed her eyes.

He divined the cause of her tears, and there was much tenderness in his utterance of the monosyllable and in the kisses he gave her. Man and wife for five years, they were still the fondest of lovers.

"My dear," said Aaron presently, "the spirit of prophecy is upon me. We shall lead a comfortable life in this town ; we shall prosper in this house. It was a piece of real good fortune my hitting upon it. When I heard by chance that the man who lived here owned the lease and wished to dispose of it, I hesitated before parting with so large a sum as a hundred pounds for the purchase. It was nearly half my capital, but I liked the look of the place, and a little bird whispered that we should be lucky in it, so I made the venture. I am certain we shall not regret it. Here shall be laid the founda-tion stones of a fortune which shall enable us to set up our carriage. I know what you would say, my life, that we can be happy without a carriage. Yes, yes ; but a carriage is not a bad thing to have. People will say, ' See what a clever man that Aaron Cohen is. He commenced with nothing, and he rides in his own carriage already. How grand he looks !' I should like to hear people say that. There is a knock at the street door."

"Who can it be?" asked Rachel. "We know no one in Gosport, and it is night."

"Which is no excuse for our not opening the door," said Aaron Cohen, sweeping the money off the table into a small chamois leather bag, which he tied carefully at the neck, and put into his pocket. "True, we believe we are not known here, but there may, nevertheless, be an old acquaintance in Gosport who has heard of our arrival, and comes to welcome us; or Judah Belasco may have told a friend of his we are here; or it may be an enterprising baker or grocer who wishes to secure our custom. No," he added, as the knock was repeated, "that is not the knock of a tradesman. It is a knock of self-importance, and you may depend upon it that it proceeds from Somebody with a large S. Let us see who it is that announces himself so grandly."

Aaron went to the street door, and Rachel followed him into the passage, carrying a candle. The night was dark, and Rachel stood a little in the rear, so that Aaron could not distinguish the features of his visitor. He was a big man, and that was all that was apparent to the Cohens.

"Mr. Cohen?" queried the visitor.

"Yes," said Aaron.

" Mr. Aaron Cohen ? "

" That is my name."

" Can I speak with you ? "

" Certainly."

And Aaron waited to hear what the stranger had to say.

" I am not accustomed to be kept waiting on the doorstep. I should prefer to speak to you in the house."

Rachel, who was naturally timid, moved closer to her husband, who took the candle from her hand, and held it up in order to see the face of the stranger.

" Step inside," he said.

The stranger followed Aaron and Rachel into the little parlour, and without taking off his hat, looked at Aaron, then at Rachel, and then into every corner of the room ; the last object upon which his eyes rested was the device of the three golden balls, and a frown gathered on his features as he gazed. Aaron noted these movements and signs with attention and amusement.

" Do you detect any blemish in them ? " he asked.

" I do not understand you," said the stranger.

"In those balls. There was an expression of disapproval on your face as you gazed at them."

"I disapprove of them altogether," said the stranger.

"I am sorry, but we cannot please everybody. I am not responsible for the insignia ; you will find the origin in the armorial bearings of the Medici. That is a beautiful hat you have on your head." The stranger stared at him. "Really," continued Aaron, blandly, "a beautiful hat ; it must have cost a guinea. A hat is a fine protection against the hot rays of the sun ; a protection, also, against the wind and the rain. But in this room, as you may observe, we have neither wind, nor rain, nor sun ; and you may also observe that there is a lady present." The stranger, reddening slightly, removed his hat, and placed it on the table. "My wife," then said Aaron.

The stranger inclined his head, with the air of a man acknowledging an introduction to one of a lower station. The manner of this acknowledgment was not lost upon Aaron.

"My wife," he repeated courteously, "Mrs. Cohen."

"I see," said the stranger, glancing again at Rachel with condescension. "With your permission I will take a seat."

It was distinctly at variance with the hospitable
instincts of Aaron Cohen that he did not immediately
respond to this request.

"You have the advantage of us," he said. "I have
had the pleasure of introducing my wife to you.
Afford me the pleasure of introducing you to
my wife."

With an ungracious air the stranger handed Aaron
a visiting card, upon which was inscribed the name
of Mr. Edward Whimpole, and in a corner the word
"Churchwarden." Mr. Whimpole's movements were
slow, and intended to be dignified, but Aaron exhibited no impatience.

"My dear, Mr. Edward Whimpole, churchwarden."

Rachel bowed gracefully, and Aaron, with an
easy motion of his hand, invited Mr. Whimpole
to a chair, in which he seated himself. Then Aaron
placed a chair for his wife, and took one himself,
and prepared to listen to what Mr. Whimpole had
to say.

Mr. Whimpole was a large-framed man with a
great deal of flesh on his face ; his eyes were light,
and he had no eyebrows worth speaking of. The
best feature in his face was his mouth, and the
most insignificant his nose, which was really not

a fair nose for a man of his bulk. It was an added injury inflicted upon him by nature that it was very thin at the end, as though it had been planed on both sides. But then, as Aaron had occasion to remark, we don't make our own noses. A distinct contrast presented itself in the two noses which, if the figure of speech may be allowed, now faced each other.

Mr. Whimpole had not disclosed the purpose of his visit, but he had already made it clear that he was not graciously disposed towards the Jew. Aaron was quite aware of this, but the only effect it had upon him was to render him exceedingly affable. Perhaps he scented a bargain, and was aware that mental irritation would interfere with the calm exercise of his judgment in a matter of buying and selling.

"May I inquire," he said, pointing to the word "churchwarden" on the card, "whether this is your business or profession?"

"I am a corn-chandler," said Mr. Whimpole.

"Churchwarden, my dear," said Aaron, addressing his wife in a pleasant tone, "*and* corn-chandler."

For the life of him Mr. Whimpole could not have explained to the satisfaction of persons not directly interested, why he was angry at the reception he was meeting. That Aaron Cohen was not the kind of man he had expected to meet would not have been accepted as a sufficient reason.

"I am not mistaken," said Mr. Whimpole, with a flush of resentment, "in believing you to be a Jew?"

"You are not mistaken," replied Aaron, with exceeding urbanity. "I am a Jew. If I were not proud of the fact, it would be folly to attempt to disguise it, for at least one feature in my face would betray me."

"It would," said Mr. Whimpole, dealing a blow which had the effect of causing Aaron to lean back in his chair, and laugh gently to himself for fully thirty seconds.

"When you have quite finished," said Mr. Whimpole, coldly, "we will proceed."

"Excuse me," said Aaron, drawing a deep breath of enjoyment. "I beg you will not consider me wanting in politeness, but I have the instincts of my race, and I never waste the smallest trifle, not even a joke." A little tuft of hair which ran down the centre of Mr. Whimpole's head—the right and left banks of which were devoid of verdure—quivered in sympathy with the proprietor's astonishment.

That a man should make a joke out of that which was generally considered to be a reproach and a humiliation was, indeed, matter for amazement; nay, in this instance for indignation, for in Aaron Cohen's laughter he, Mr. Whimpole himself, was made to occupy a ridiculous place. "We are loth," continued Aaron, "to waste even the thinnest joke. We are at once, my dear sir, both thrifty and liberal."

"We!" exclaimed Mr. Whimpole, in hot repudiation.

"We Jews I mean. No person in the world could possibly mistake you for one of the chosen."

"I should hope not. The idea is too absurd."

"Make your mind easy, sir; you would not pass muster in a synagogue without exciting remark. Yes, we are both thrifty and liberal, wasting nothing, and in the free spending of our money seeing that we get good value for it. That is not a reproach, nor is it a reproach that we thoroughly enjoy an agreeable thing when we get it for nothing. There are so many things in life to vex us that the opportunity of a good laugh should never be neglected. Proceed, my dear sir, proceed; you were saying that you believed you were not mistaken in taking me for a Jew."

"Is it your intention," asked Mr. Whimpole, coming now straight to the point, "to reside in Gosport?"

"If I am permitted," replied Aaron, meekly. "We have not always been allowed to select our place of residence. I am thankful that we live in an enlightened age and in a free country."

"I hear, Mr. Cohen, that you have purchased the lease of this house."

"It is true, sir. The purchase money has been paid, and the lease is mine."

"It has twenty-seven years to run."

"Twenty-seven years and three months. Who can tell where we shall be, and how we shall be situated, at the end of that time?"

Mr. Whimpole waved the contemplation aside. "You gave a hundred pounds for the lease."

"The precise sum; your information is correct."

"I had some intention, Mr. Cohen, of buying it myself."

"Indeed! Why did you not do so?"

"There were reasons. Not pecuniary, I beg to say. I delayed too long, and you stepped in before me."

"A case of the early bird catching the worm," Aaron observed, with a smile.

" If it gratifies you to put it that way. I have, therefore, no option but to purchase the lease of you."

" Mr. Whimpole," said Aaron, after a slight pause, " I am agreeable to sell you the lease."

" I thought as much." And Mr. Whimpole disposed himself comfortably in his chair.

Rachel's eyes dilated in surprise. Their settlement in Gosport had not been made in haste, and all arrangements for commencing the business were made. She could not understand her husband's willingness to give up the house.

" I do not expect you to take what you gave for it," said Mr. Whimpole. " I am prepared to give you a profit ; and," he added, jocosely, " you will not be backward in accepting it."

" Not at all backward. You speak like a man of sense."

" How much do you ask for your bargain ? How much, Mr. Cohen ? Don't open your mouth too wide."

" If you will permit me," said Aaron, and he proceeded to pencil down a calculation. " It is not an undesirable house, Mr. Whimpole."

" No, no ; I don't say it is."

" It is compact and convenient."

" Fairly so, fairly so."

" I will accept," said Aaron, having finished his calculation, " five hundred pounds."

" You cannot be in earnest!" gasped Mr. Whimpole, his breath fairly taken away.

"I am quite in earnest. Are you aware what it is you would buy of me ? "

" Of course I am aware ; the lease of this house."

" Not that alone. You would buy my hopes for the next twenty-seven years ; for I declare to you there is not to my knowledge in all England a spot in which I so desire to pass my days as in this peaceful town ; and there is not in all Gosport a house in which I believe I shall be so happy as in this. You see, you propose to purchase of me something more than a parchment lease."

" But the—the things you mention are of no value to me."

" I do not say they are. I am speaking from my point of view, as men generally do. It is a failing we all have, Mr. Whimpole. There is no reason why we should bandy words. I am not anxious to sell the lease. Wait till it is in the market."

"A most unhealthy situation," observed Mr. Whimpole.

" It concerns ourselves, and we are contented."

" I cannot imagine a more unpleasant, not to say obnoxious, view."

"The view of the churchyard? The spot has already acquired an inestimable value in my eyes. God rest the souls of those who lie in it! The contemplation of the peaceful ground will serve to remind me of the vanity of life, and will be a constant warning to me to be fair and straightforward in my dealings. The warning may be needed, for in the business I intend to carry on, there are—I do not deny it—many dangerous temptations."

" Tush, tush!" exclaimed Mr. Whimpole, petulantly. " Straightforward dealings, indeed! The vanity of life, indeed!" '

Aaron Cohen smiled.

Only once before in his life had Mr. Whimpole felt so thoroughly uncomfortable as at the present moment, and that was when he was a little boy and fell into a bed of nettles from which he was unable to extricate himself until he was covered with stings. It was just the same now ; he was smarting all over from contact with Aaron Cohen,

who was like a porcupine with sharp-pointed quills.
But he would not tamely submit to such treatment ;
he would show Aaron that he could sting in return ;
he knew well enough where to plant his poisoned
arrow.

It is due to Mr. Whimpole to state that he was
not aware that the manner in which he was con-
ducting himself during this interview was not com-
mendable.   Being a narrow-minded man, he could
not take a wide and generous view of abstract
matters, which, by a perversion of reasoning, he
generally regarded from a purely personal standpoint.
Such men as he, in their jealous regard for their
own feelings, are apt to overlook the feelings of
others, and, indeed, to behave occasionally as if
they did not possess any.   This was Mr. Whimpole's
predicament, and, having met a ready-witted man,
he was made to suffer for his misconduct.   He
sent forth his sting in this wise :

"You speak, Mr. Cohen, of being fair and straightforward in your dealings ; but, for the matter of
that, we all know what we may expect from a——"

And having got thus far in his ungenerously-
prompted speech, he felt himself unable, in the presence of Rachel, and with her reproachful eyes

raised to his face, to conclude the sentence. Aaron
Cohen finished it for him.

"For the matter of that," he said, gently, "you
all know what you may expect from a Jew. That
is what you were going to say. And with this
thought in your mind you came to trade with me.
Well, sir, it may be that we both have something
to learn."

"Mr. Cohen," said Mr. Whimpole, slightly abashed,
"I am sorry if I have said anything to hurt your
feelings."

"The offence, sir, is atoned for by the expression
of your sorrow."

This was taking high ground, and Mr. Whimpole's
choler was ready to rise again; but he mastered
it, and said, in a conciliatory tone,—

"I will disguise nothing from you; I was born
in this house."

"The circumstance will make it all the more
valuable to us. My dear,"—impressing it upon
Rachel with pleasant emphasis—"Mr. Whimpole
was born in this house. A fortunate omen. Good
luck will come to us, as it has come to him. It
is a low-rented house, and those who have been
born in it must have been poor men's children.

When they rise in the world as Mr. Whimpole has
done, it is better than a horseshoe over the door.
In which room were you born, Mr. Whimpole?"

"In the room on the back of the first floor,"
replied Mr. Whimpole, making a wild guess.

"Our bedroom. There should be a record on the
walls ; there should, indeed, be a record, such as
is placed outside those houses in London which have
been inhabited by famous people. Failing that, it
is 'in the power of every man, assuredly every rich
man, to make for himself a record that shall be
unperishable—far better, my dear sir, than the mere
fixing of a plate on a cold stone wall."

Mr. Whimpole gazed at Aaron Cohen to discover
if there was any trace of mockery in his face ; but
Aaron was perfectly grave and serious.

"A man's humility," said Mr. Whimpole, raising
his eyes to the ceiling, "his sense of humbleness,
would prevent him from making this record for
himself. It has to be left to others to do it when
they have found him out."

"Aha! my dear sir," said Aaron, softly, "when
they have found him out. True, true ; but how
few of us are! How few of us receive our just
reward! How few of us when we are in our graves

receive or deserve the tribute, 'Here lies a perfect man!' But the record I speak of will never be lost by a rich man's humility, by his humbleness; for it can be written unostentatiously in the hearts of the poor by the aid of silver and gold."

"I understand you, Mr. Cohen,"—inwardly confounding Aaron's flow of ideas—"by means of charity."

"Yes, sir, by means of charity, whereby the name of a man becomes sweet in the mouth. A good name is better than precious oil, and the day of one's death better than the day of his birth. There is an old legend that a man's actions in life are marked in the air above him, in the places in which they are performed. There, in invisible space, are inscribed the records of his good and bad deeds, of his virtues, of his crimes; and when he dies his soul visits those places, and views the immortal writing, which is visible to all the angels in heaven, and which covers him with shame or glory. Gosport doubtless has many such records of your charity."

"I do my best," said Mr. Whimpole, very much confused and mystified; "I hope I do my best. I said I would disguise nothing from you; I will therefore be quite frank, with no intention of wound-

ing you.   I am strictly a religious man, Mr. Cohen,
and it hurts me that one whose religious belief is
opposed to my own should inhabit the house in
which I was born.   I will give you a hundred and
twenty pounds for the lease ; that will leave you a
profit of twenty pounds.   Come, now ! "

"I will not accept less for it, sir, than the sum
I named."

" Is that your last word ? "

" It is my last word."

Mr. Whimpole rose with a face of scarlet, and
clapped his hat on his head.

"You are a—a—— "

"A Jew.   Leave it at that.   Can you call me
anything worse ? " asked Aaron, with no show of
anger.

" No, I cannot.   You are a Jew."

" I regret," said Aaron, calmly, " that I cannot
retort by calling you a Christian.   May our next
meeting be more agreeable !   Good-evening, Mr.
Whimpole."

"You do not know the gentleman you have
insulted," said Mr. Whimpole, as he walked towards
the door ; "you do not know my position in this
town.   I am in the expectation of being made a

justice of the peace. You will live to repent this."

" I think not," said Aaron, taking the candle to show his visitor out. " I trust you may."

" You may find your residence in Gosport, where I am universally respected, not as agreeable as you would wish it to be."

" We shall see, we shall see," said Aaron, still smiling. " I may also make myself respected here."

" There is a prejudice against your race—— "

" Am I not aware of it? Is not every Jew aware of it? Is it not thrown in our teeth by the bigoted and narrow-minded upon every possible occasion? We will live it down, sir. We have already done much ; we will yet do more. Your use of the word ' prejudice ' is appropriate ; for, as I understand its meaning, it represents a judgment formed without proper knowledge. Yes, sir, it is not to be disputed that there exists a prejudice against our race."

" Which, without putting any false meaning upon it, will make this ancient and respectable town "— here Mr. Whimpole found himself at a loss, and he was compelled to wind up with the vulgar figure of speech—" too hot to hold you."

" This ancient town," said Aaron, with a deeper

seriousness in his voice, "is known to modern men as Gosport."

" A clever discovery," sneered Mr. Whimpole. " Are you going to put another of your false constructions on it ? "

" No, sir. I am about to tell you a plain and beautiful truth. When in olden times a name was given to this place, it was not Gosport : it was God's Port ; and what God's port is there throughout the civilised world in which Jew and Christian alike have not an equal right to live, despite prejudice, despite bigotry, and despite the unreasonable anger of large corn-chandlers and respected churchwardens ? I wish you, sir, good-night."

And having by this time reached the street door, Aaron Cohen opened it for Mr. Whimpole, and bowed him politely out.

CHAPTER XII.

THE COURSE OF THE SEASONS.

UPON Aaron's return to the little parlour he saw that Rachel was greatly disturbed.

" My life !" he said, and he folded her in his arms and tenderly embraced her. " Don't allow such a little thing as this to distress you ; it will all come right in the end."

" But how you kept your temper," she said ; " that is what surprised me."

" It gave me the advantage of him, Rachel. I was really amused."

He pinched her cheeks to bring the colour back to them.

" Some men must be managed one way, some another. And now for our game of bezique. Mr. Whimpole's visit "—he laughed at the recollection— " will make me enjoy it all the more."

There was no resisting his light-heartedness, and he won a smile from her, despite her anxiety.

Rachel was not clever enough to discover that it was only by the cunning of her husband that she won the rub of bezique. He was a keen judge of human nature, and he knew that this small victory would help to soothe her.

The next day was Friday, and the three golden balls were put up, and the name of Aaron Cohen painted over the shop door. A great many people came to look, and departed to circulate the news.

At one o'clock the painting was done, and then Aaron said to his wife, "I shall be out till the evening. Have you found any one to attend to the lights and the fire ? "

They were not rich enough to keep a regular servant, and neither of them ever touched fire on the Sabbath.

" I have heard of a woman," said Rachel ; " she is coming this afternoon to see me."

" Good," said Aaron, and, kissing Rachel, went away with a light heart.

In the afternoon the woman, Mrs. Hawkins, called, and Rachel explained the nature of the services she required. Mrs. Hawkins was to come to the house every Friday night to put coals on the fire and extinguish the lights, and four times on Saturday to

perform the same duties. Rachel proposed eightpence a week, but Mrs. Hawkins stuck out for tenpence,
and this being acceded to, she departed, leaving a
strong flavour of gin behind her.

When Aaron returned, the two Sabbath candles
were alight upon the snow-white tablecloth, and on
the table a supper was spread—fried fish, white bread,
and fresh butter, and in the fender a steaming coffee-
pot. Rachel was an excellent cook, and had always
been famous for her fried and stewed fish, which her
husband declared were dishes fit for kings ; and, indeed, no one in the land could have desired tastier
or more succulent cooking.

Aaron washed and said his prayers, and then they
sat down to their meal in a state of perfect content-
ment. The head of the modest household broke two
small pieces of bread from the loaf, and dipping them
in salt, besought the customary blessing on the bread
they were about to eat ; then praised the fish, praised
the butter, praised the coffee, praised his wife, and
after a full meal praised the Lord, in a Song of
Degrees, for blessings received : " When the Eternal
restored the captivity of Zion, we were as those who
dream. Our mouths were then filled with laughter,
and our tongues with song."

He had a rich baritone voice, and Rachel listened in pious delight to his intoning of the prayer. The supper things were cleared away, the white tablecloth being allowed to remain because of the lighted candles on it, which it would have been breaking the Sabbath to lift, and then there came a knock at the street door.

"That is the woman I engaged," said Rachel, hurrying into the passage.

There entered, not Mrs. Hawkins, but a very small girl, carrying a very large baby. The baby might have been eighteen months old, and the girl ten years; and of the twain the baby was the plumper.

Without "With your leave" or "By your leave," the small girl pushed past Rachel before the astonished woman could stop her, and presented herself before the no less astonished Aaron Cohen. Her sharp eyes took in the lighted candles, the cheerful fire, and the master of the house in one comprehensive flash. With some persons what is known as making up one's mind is a slow and complicated process, with the small girl it was electrical. She deposited the large baby in Aaron's lap, admonishing the infant "to keep quiet, or she'd ketch it," blew out the candles in two swift puffs, and, kneeling before the grate, proceeded to rake out the coals. So rapid were her movements that the fender was half filled with cinders and blazing coals before Rachel had time to reach the room.

"In Heaven's name," cried Aaron, "what is the meaning of this?"

"It's all right, sir," said the small girl, in the dark ; " I've come for aunty."

"Put down the poker instantly!" exclaimed Aaron. "Your aunty, whoever she may be, is not here."

"Tell me somethink I don't know," requested the small girl. "This is Mr. Cohen's, the Jew, ain't it?"

"It is," replied Aaron, with despairing gestures, for the baby was dabbing his face with hands sticky with remnants of sugarstuff.

"Well, wot are yer 'ollering for? I'm only doing wot aunty told me."

"And who *is* your aunty?"

"Mrs. 'Orkins. Pretend not to know 'er—do! Oh yes, jest you try it on. Aunty's up to yer, she is. She sed yer'd try to do 'er out of 'er money, and want 'er to take fippence instid of tenpence."

"Did she? You have come here by her orders, I suppose?"

"Yes, I 'ave ; to poke out the fire and blow out the candles, and I've done it."

"You have," said Aaron, ruefully. "And now, little girl, you will do as *I* tell you. Put down that poker. Get up. Feel on the mantelshelf for a box of matches. I beg your pardon, you are too short to reach. Here is the box. Take out a match. Strike it. Light the candles. Thank you. Last, but not least, relieve me of this baby with the sticky hands."

The small girl snatched the baby from his arms and stood before him in an attitude of defiance. For the first time he had a clear view of her.

"Heaven save us!" he cried, falling back in his chair.

Her appearance was a sufficient explanation of his astonishment. To say that she was ragged, and dirty, and forlorn, and as utterly unlike a little girl living in civilised society as any little girl could possibly be, would be but a poor description of her. Her face suggested that she had been lying with her head in a coal scuttle ; she wore no hat or bonnet ; her hair was matted ; her frock reached just below her knees, and might have been picked out of a dust-heap ; she had no stockings ; on her feet were two odd boots, several sizes too large for her and quite worn out, one tied to her ankle with a piece of grey list, the other similarly secured with a piece of knotted twine. Her eyes glittered with preternatural sharpness ; her cheek bones stuck out ; her elbows were pointed and red ; she was all bone—literally all bone ; there was not an ounce of flesh upon her, not any part of her body that could be pinched with a sense of satisfaction. But the baby ! What a contrast ! Her head was round and chubby, and was covered with a mass of light curls ; her hands were full of dimples ; her face was puffed out with superabundant flesh ; the calves of her legs were a picture. In respect of clothes she was no better off than Mrs. Hawkins's niece.

"Wot are yer staring at ? " demanded the girl.

" At you, my child," replied Aaron, with compassion in his voice.

" Let's know when yer done," retorted the girl, "and I'll tell yer wot I charge for it."

" And at baby," added Aaron.

" That'll be hextra. Don't say I didn't warn yer."

There were conflicting elements in the situation ; its humour was undeniable, but it had its pathetic side. Aaron Cohen was swayed now by one emotion, now by another.

"So you are Mrs. Hawkins's niece," he said, with a twinkle in his eyes.

"Yes, I am. Wot 'ave yer got to say agin it?"

"Nothing. Is baby also Mrs. Hawkins's niece, or nephew?"

"If you've no objections," said the girl, with excessive politeness, "she's Mrs. Pond's little gal, and I nusses 'er."

"I have no objection. What is your name?"

"Wot it may be, my lordship," replied the girl, her politeness becoming Arctic, "is one thing—wot it is, is another."

"You are a clever little girl," said Aaron, smiling and rubbing his hands, "a sharp, clever little girl."

"Thank yer for nothink," said the girl.

She had reached the North Pole; it was necessary to thaw her.

"Upon the mantelshelf," said Aaron, "just behind that beautiful blue vase, are two penny pieces. Step on a chair—not that cane one, you'll go through it; the wooden one—and see if you can find them."

"I see 'em," said the girl, looking down upon Aaron in more senses than one.

"They are yours. Put them in your pocket."

The girl clutched the pennies, jumped from the

chair—whereat the baby crowed, supposing it to be a game provided for her amusement—and having no pocket, held the money tight in her hand. Visions of sweetstuff rose before her. The pennies getting warm, the ice in the North Pole began to melt. But there was a doubt in the girl's mind ; the adventure was almost too good to be true.

" Yer don't get 'em back," she said ; " stow larks, yer know."

" I don't want them back. And now, perhaps, you will tell me your name."

" Prissy. That's the short 'un."

" The long one is——"

" Priscilla."

" A grand name. You ought to have a silk gown, and satin shoes, and a gold comb." Prissy opened her eyes very wide. The ice was melting quickly, and the buds were coming on the trees. " And baby's name ? "

" Wictoria Rejiner. That's grander, ain't it ? "

" Much grander. Victoria Regina—a little queen ! " Prissy gave baby a kiss, with pride and love in her glittering eyes. " What makes your face so black, Prissy ? "

" Coals. Aunty deals in 'em, and ginger-beer, and

bundles of wood, and cabbages, and taters, and oranges, and lemons. And she takes in washing."

"You look, Prissy, as if you had very little to eat."

So genial was Aaron Cohen's voice that spring was coming on fast.

"I don't 'ave much," said Prissy, with a longing sigh. "I could eat all day and night if I 'ad the chance."

"My dear," said Aaron to his wife, "there is some coffee left in the pot. Do you like coffee, Prissy?"

"Do I like corfey? Don't I like corfey! Oh no— not me! Jest you try me!"

"I will. Give me Victoria Regina. Poke the fire. That's right; you are the quickest, sharpest little girl in my acquaintance. Pour some water from the kettle into the coffee-pot. Set it on the fire. Rachel, my dear, take Prissy and baby into the kitchen and let them wash themselves, and afterwards they shall have some supper."

The buds were breaking into blossom ; it really was a lovely spring.

In a few minutes Rachel and the children re-entered the room from the kitchen, baby with a clean face, and Prissy with a painfully red and shining skin. Following her husband's instructions, Rachel cut half-a-dozen slices of bread, upon which she spread the butter with a liberal hand. Prissy, hugging Victoria Regina, watched the proceedings in silence. By this time the coffee was bubbling in the pot.

"Take it off the fire, Prissy," said Aaron Cohen ; and in another minute the little girl, with baby in her lap, was sitting at the table with a cup of smoking hot coffee, well sugared and milked, which she was so eager to drink that she scalded her throat. The bread and butter was perhaps the sweetest that Prissy had ever eaten, and the coffee was nectar. The baby ate more than Prissy ; indeed, she ate so much and so quickly that she occasionally choked and had to be violently shaken and patted on the back, but she became tired out at last, and before Prissy had finished her bounteous meal she was fast asleep in her nurse's arms.

Aaron Cohen leaned back in his chair, and gazed with benevolent eyes upon the picture before him ; and as he gazed the sweetest of smiles came to his lips, and did not leave them. Rachel, stealing to the back of his chair, put her arms round his neck, and nestled her face to his.

It was a most beautiful summer, and all the trees were in flower.

CHAPTER XIII.

AARON COHEN PREACHES A SERMON ON LARGE NOSES.

THE fire was burning brightly, and the old cat which they had brought with them to Gosport was stretched at full length upon the hearthrug. The children were gone, and Prissy had received instructions to come again at ten o'clock to extinguish the candles. It may be said of Prissy, in respect of her first visit to the house, that she came in like a lion and went out like a lamb.

It was a habit on Sabbath eve for Aaron to read to his wife something from the general literature of the times, or from the newspapers, and to accompany his reading with shrewd or sympathetic remarks, to which Rachel always listened in delight. Occasionally he read from a book of Hebrew prayers, and commented upon them, throwing a light upon poem and allegory which made their meaning clear to Rachel's understanding. Invariably, also, he blessed her as

Jewish fathers who have not wandered from the paths of orthodoxy bless their children on the Sabbath. Now, as she stood before him, he placed his hand on her head, and said,—

"God make thee like Sarah, Rebecca, Rachel, and Leah. May the Eternal bless and preserve thee! May the Eternal cause His face to shine upon thee, and be gracious unto thee! May the Eternal lift up His countenance towards thee, and grant thee peace!"

It was something more than a blessing; it was a prayer of heartfelt love. Rachel raised her face to his, and they tenderly kissed each other. Then he took his seat on one side of the fire, and she on the other. A prayer-book and one of Charles Dickens's stories were on the table, but he did not open them; he had matter for thought, and he was in the mood for conversation. He was in a light humour, which exhibited itself in a quiet laugh, which presently deepened in volume.

"I am thinking of the little girl," he explained to Rachel. "It was amazing the way she puffed out the candles and poked out the fire—quick as lightning. It was the most comical thing! And her black face— and Victoria Regina's sticky fingers! Ha, ha, ha!"

His merriment was contagious, and it drew forth Rachel's ; the room was filled with pleasant sound.

"I saw Mr. Whimpole to-day," said Aaron, "and I made him a bow, which he did not return. My Jewish nose offends him. How unfortunate! Yes, my life, no one can dispute that the Jew has a big nose. It proclaims itself ; it is a mark and a sign. He himself often despises it ; he himself often looks at it in the glass with aversion. 'Why, why, have I been compelled to endure this affliction?' he murmurs, and he reflects with envy upon the elegant nose of the Christian. Short-sighted mortal, not to understand that he owes everything to his big nose! A great writer—a learned man, who passed the whole of his life in the study of these matters—proclaims the nose to be the foundation, or abutment, of the brain. What follows? That the larger is the nose of a man, the better off for it is the man. Listen, my dear." He took a book from a little nest of bookshelves, and turned over the pages. "'Whoever,' says this learned writer, 'is acquainted with the Gothic arch will perfectly understand what I mean by this abutment; for upon this the whole power of the arch of the forehead rests, and without it the mouth and cheeks would be oppressed by miserable ruins.' He lays down exact laws, which govern the beautiful (and therefore the large) nose. Its length should equal the length of the forehead, the back should be broad, its outline remarkably definite, the sides well defined, and, near the eye, it must be at least half an inch in breadth. Such a nose, this great authority declares, is of more worth than a kingdom. It imparts solidity and unity to the whole countenance; it is the mountain—bear in mind, my dear, the mountain—that shelters the fair vales beneath. How proud, then, should I be of my nose, which in some respects answers to this description! Not in all, no, not in all. I am not so vain as to believe that my nose is worth more than a kingdom; but when I am told that a large nose is a sign of sensibility, and of good nature and good humour, I cannot help a glow of conceited satisfaction stealing over me. How many great men have you known with small noses? There are, of course, exceptions, but I speak of the general rule. Our co-religionist, Benjamin Disraeli—look at his nose; look at the noses of all our great Jewish musicians and composers —it is because they are of a proper size that they have become famous. Some time since in London I had the opportunity of looking over a wonderful

Bible—six enormous volumes published by Mr.
Thomas Macklin nearly a century ago—embellished
with grand pictures by the most eminent English
artists ; and there I saw the figures of Abraham and
Isaac and Jacob, and other ancestors of ours.   There
is not a small nose on one of the faces of these great
patriarchs and prophets.   The great painters who
drew them had learned from their studies how to
delineate the biblical heroes.   Moses the law-giver—
what an administrator, what a grand general was
that hero, my dear !   How thoroughly he understood
men and human nature !   Aaron, the high priest ;
King Solomon, the man of wisdom ; Isaiah, the
prophet and poet—they all had tremendous noses.
A big nose is a grand decoration, and I would sooner
possess it than a bit of red ribbon in my button-hole,
or a star on my breast.   Indeed, my life, I have it—
the nose of my forefathers !"   Aaron made this
declaration in a tone of comic despair.   " And, having
it, I will not part with it except with life."

There was so much playful humour in the dis-
sertation that Rachel laughed outright.   Her laugh
was the sweetest in the world, and it fell like music
on Aaron's heart.   He smiled, and there was a gleam
in his eyes, and presently he spoke again.

" I am not aware whether you have ever observed the attraction a big nose has for children. Take the most popular drama of all ages, ' Punch and Judy.' Where is the artist who would venture to present Punch with any but an enormous nose? Are the children frightened at it? No, they revel in it. Do they sympathise with Judy when she is slain? Not at all; every whack Punch gives her is greeted with shrieks of laughter—because of his enormous nose. Introduce two strangers to a baby, one with a very small nose, the other with a very big nose. Let them both hold out their arms. Instinctively the baby flies to the man with the large nose. It is nature's silent voice that instructs the child. He or she—the sex is not material—instinctively knows which is the better nose of the two, which is the most promising nose, the most suggestive of kisses, and jumps in the air, and cakes, and songs, and all that is dear to a child's heart. The test is infallible. Nothing will convince me that you did not marry me because of my big nose."

" Indeed, dear," said Rachel, still laughing, " I hardly think I would have married you without it."

" Then the fact is established. I am about to make a confession to you, Rachel; I am going to

tell you the true reason for my choosing this place
to reside in, where I am separated by a long distance
from the friends of my youth and manhood, and
where you, too, my dear child"—in his moments
of tenderness he occasionally addressed her thus—
"will, I fear, be for a time without friends to whom
you can unbosom yourself."

"I have you, my dear husband," said Rachel,
in a tone of deep affection, drawing closer to him,
and slipping her little hand into his great hand.
A fine, large, nervous hand was Aaron Cohen's; a
palmister would have seen great possibilities in it.
Rachel's hand, despite her domestic work, was the
hand of a lady; she took a proper pride in preserving
its delicacy and beauty. "I have you, my dear
husband," she said.

"Yes, my life, but you used to kiss at least a
dozen female friends a day."

"I kissed Prissy and the baby to-night."

"When their faces were washed, I hope. Listen
to my confession. Pride and hard-heartedness drove
me from the neighbourhood in which we were
married. A thousand pounds did my dear father—
God rest his soul!—bequeath to me. It dwindled
and dwindled—my own fault; I could not say No.

One came to me with a melancholy tale which led to a little loan ; another came, and another, and another. I did not make you acquainted with the extent of my transgressions. My dear, I encouraged the needy ones ; I even went out of my way to lend, thinking myself a fine fellow, and flapping my wings in praise of my stupidity. Not half I lent came back to me. Then business began to fall off, and I saw that I was in the wrong groove. I had grown into bad ways ; and had I remained much longer in the old neighbourhood I should have been left without a penny. I thought of our future, of the injustice I was inflicting upon you. ' I will go,' said I, ' where I am not known, while I still have a little to earn a living with, among strangers who, when they borrow, will give me value in return, and where I shall not have to say to poor friends, " Come to me no more ; I am poorer than yourselves." I have been foolish and weak ; I will be wise and strong. I will grow rich and hard-hearted.' Yes, my dear, that is what I intend, and my heart will not be oppressed by the sight of suffering it is out of my power to relieve. Rachel, I am not so clever as I pretend to be ; to speak the truth, I am afraid I am rather given to crowing ; and when it is not alone my own welfare, but the welfare of one so dear to me as you are, that is concerned, I tremble, I begin to doubt whether I have done right. Give me your opinion of the step I have taken."

She gazed at him with serious, loving, trustful eyes. "It is a wise step, Aaron, I am sure it is. Whatever you do is right, and I am satisfied."

Ten o'clock struck, and a knock at the door announced the faithful Prissy, come to put the fire out. She entered with the baby in her arms, sound asleep. She was flushed and excited, and she held her hand over the right side of her face.

"Victoria ought to be a-bed," said Rachel, taking a peep at baby.

"She can't go," retorted Prissy, "afore 'er mother's ready to take 'er."

"Where is her mother?" asked Aaron.

"At the Jolly Sailor Boy, enjying of 'erself."

"Ah! And where is your aunt?"

"At the Jolly Sailor Boy, too, 'aving a 'arf-quartern. There's been a reg'lar row there about Mrs. Macrory's flannin peddicut."

"What happened to it?"

"It went wrong. Yes, it did. Yer needn't larf. Call me a story, do! I would if I was you!"

" No, no, Prissy," said Aaron, in a soothing tone.
" How did the flannel petticoat go wrong ? "

" Nobody knowed at fust.   Aunty does Mrs.
Macrory's washing, and a lot more besides, and the
things gits mixed sometimes.   Aunty can't 'elp that
—'ow can she ?   So Mrs. Macrory's things was took
'ome without the peddicut.   Mrs. Macrory she meets
aunty at the Jolly Sailor Boy, and she begins to
kick up about it.   ' Where's my flannin peddicut ? '
she ses.   ' 'Ow should I know ? ' ses aunty.   Then
wot d'yer think ?   Mrs. Macrory sees somethink
sticking out of aunty's dress be'ind, and she pulls at
it.   ' Why,' she ses, ' you've got it on ! '   That's wot
the row was about.   Aunty didn't know 'ow it come
on 'er—she's ready to take 'er oath on that.   Ain't
it rum ? "

" Very rum.   Put out the fire, Prissy.   It is time
for all good people to get to bed."

In the performance of this duty Prissy was compelled to remove her hand from her face, and when
she rose from the floor it was seen that her right eye
was sadly discoloured, and that she was in pain.

" Oh, Prissy, poor child ! " exclaimed Rachel ; " you
have been hurt ! "

" Yes, mum," said Prissy.   " Mrs. Macrory's gal

—she's twice as big as me ; you should see 'er legs !
—she ses, 'You're in that job,' she ses, meaning
the peddicut ; and she lets fly and gives me a one-er
on account."

Rachel ran upstairs, and brought down a bottle of
gillard water, with which she bathed the bruise, and
tied one of her clean white handkerchiefs over it.
Prissy stood quite still, her lips quivering ; it may
have been the gillard water that filled the girl's
unbandaged eye with tears.

"That will make you feel easier," said Rachel.
" Blow out the candles now, and be here at half-past
eight in the morning."

" I'll be sure to be," said Prissy, with a shake in
her voice.

In the dark Aaron Cohen heard the sound of a
kiss.

" Good-night, sir," said the girl.

" Good-night, Prissy," said Aaron.

The chain of the street door was put up, and
the shutters securely fastened, and then Aaron and
Rachel, hand in hand, went up the dark stairs to
their room.

" My dear," said Aaron, drowsily, a few minutes
after he and his wife were in bed, " are you asleep ? "

"No, Aaron," murmured Rachel, who was on the border-land of dreams.

"I've been thinking,"—he dozed off for a moment or two—"I've been thinking——"

"Yes, my dear?"

—"That I wouldn't give Prissy's aunt any flannel petticoats to wash."

Almost before the words had passed his lips sleep claimed him for its own.

CHAPTER XIV.

A PROCLAMATION OF WAR.

ON Monday morning Aaron commenced business. In the shop window was a display of miscellaneous articles ticketed at low prices, and Aaron took his place behind his counter, ready to dispose of them, ready to argue and bargain, and to advance money on any other articles on which a temporary loan was required. He did not expect a rush of customers, being aware that pawnbroking was a tree of very small beginnings, a seed which needed time before it put forth flourishing branches. The security was sure, the profits accumulative. He was confident of the result. Human necessity, even human frailty, was on his side; all he had to do was to be fair in his dealings.

In the course of the day he had a good many callers ; some to make inquiries, some to offer various articles for pledge. Of these latter the majority were children, with whom he declined to negotiate. "Who sent you ? " " Mother." " Go home and tell her she must come herself." He would only do business with grown-up people. Setting before himself a straight and honest rule of life, he was not the man to wander from it for the sake of a little profit. Of the other description of callers a fair proportion entered the shop out of idle curiosity. He had pleasant words for all, and gave change for sixpences and shillings with as much courtesy as if each transaction was a gain to him ; as, indeed, it was, for no man or woman who entered with an unfavourable opinion of him (influenced by certain rumours to his discredit which had been circulated by Mr. Whimpole) departed without having their minds disturbed by his urbanity and genial manners. "I don't see any harm in him," was the general verdict from personal evidence ; " he's as nice a spoken man as I ever set eyes on." Many of his visitors went away laughing at the humorous remarks he had made, which they passed on from one to another. On the evening of this first day he expressed his satisfaction at the business he had done.

" Our venture will turn out well," he said to Rachel. " The flag of fortune is waving over us."

It was eight o'clock, and, although he scarcely

expected further custom, he kept the gas burning in the shop window.

" Light is an attraction," he observed. " It is better than an advertisement in the papers."

The evening was fine. He and Rachel were sitting in the parlour, with the intermediate door open. Aaron was smoking a handsome silver-mounted pipe and making up his accounts, while his wife was busy with her needle. Satan could never have put anything in the shape of mischief in the way of these two pairs of industrious hands, for they were never idle, except during the Sabbath and the fasts and holydays, and then it was not idleness, but rest, Divinely ordained. The silver-mounted pipe was one of Aaron's most precious possessions, it being his beloved wife's gift to him on his last birthday. He would not have sold it for ten times its weight in gold. Rachel often held a light to it after it was filled, and Aaron, with an affectionate smile, would kiss her white hand in acknowledgment of the service. There are trifling memorials which are almost human in their influence, and in the tender thoughts they inspire. At peace with the world and with themselves, Aaron and his wife conversed happily as they worked; but malignant influences were at work, of which they were soon to feel the shock.

Aaron had put his account books in the safe, and was turning the key, when the sound of loud voices outside his shop reached their ears. The voices were those of children, male and female, who were exercising their lungs in bass, treble, and falsetto. Only one word did they utter.

" Jew ! Jew ! Jew ! "

Rachel started up in alarm, her hand at her heart. Her face was white, her limbs were trembling.

" Jew ! Jew ! Jew ! "

Aaron put the key of the safe in his pocket, and laid down his pipe. His countenance was not troubled, but his brows were puckered.

" Jew ! Jew ! Jew ! "

" It is wicked ! it is wicked ! " cried Rachel, wringing her hands. " Oh, how can they be so cruel ! "

Aaron's countenance instantly cleared. He had to think, to act, for her as well as for himself. With fond endearments he endeavoured to soothe her ; but her agitation was profound, and while these cries of implied opprobrium continued she could not school herself to calmness. Not for herself did she fear ;

it was against her dear, her honoured husband that
this wicked demonstration was made, and she dreaded
that he would be subjected to violence. Stories
of past oppressions, accounts she had read in the
newspapers of Jew-baiting in other countries, flashed
into her mind. To her perturbed senses the voices
seemed to proceed from men and women ; to
Aaron's clearer senses they were the voices of
children, and he divined the source of the insult.
Rachel sobbed upon his breast, and clasped him
close to protect him.

"Rachel, my love, my life!" he said, in a tone
of tender firmness. "Be calm, I entreat you. There
is nothing to fear. Have you lost confidence in
your husband? Would you increase my troubles,
and make the task before me more difficult than
it is? On my word as a man, on my faith as a
Jew, I will make friends of these foolish children,
in whose outcries there is no deep-seated venom—
I declare it, none. They do not know what they
are doing. From my heart I pity them, the young
rascals, and I will wage a peaceful war with them
—yes, my life, a peaceful war—which will confound
them and fill them with wonder. I will make them
respect me ; I will enrich them with a memory which,

when they are men and women, will make them think of the past with shame. I will make all my enemies respect me. If you will help me by your silence and patience, I will turn their bitterness into thistledown, which I can blow away with a breath. Take heart, my beloved, dear life of my life! Trust to me, and in the course of a few days you shall see a wonder. There, let me kiss your tears away. That is my own Rachel, whose little finger is more precious to me than all the world beside. Good, good, my own dear wife! Do you think it is a tragedy that is being enacted by those youngsters? No, no; it is a comedy. You shall see, you shall see!"

She was comforted by his words; she drew strength from his strength; she looked at him in wonder, as he began to laugh even while he was caressing her, and her wonder increased when she saw that his eyes fairly shone with humour.

"Have no fear, my heart," he said; "have not the slightest fear. I am going to meet them—not with javelin and spear, but with something still more powerful, and with good temper for my shield."

"Aaron," she whispered, "are you sure there is no danger?"

"If I were not sure," he answered, merrily, "I would remain snug in this room. I am not a man of war; I am a man of peace, and with peaceful weapons will I scatter the enemy. For your dear sake I would not expose myself to peril, for do I not know that if I were hurt your pain would be greater than mine? It is my joy to know it. You will remain quietly here?"

"I will, my dear husband. But you will not go into the street?"

"I shall go no farther than the street door. I shall not need to go farther."

He stopped to fill his pipe, and to light it; and then, with loving kisses and a smile on his lips, he left her.

When he made his appearance at the shop door there was a sudden hush, and a sudden scuttling away of the twenty or thirty children who had congregated to revile him. He remained stationary at the door, smoking his pipe, and gazing benignantly at them.

Their fears of chastisement dispelled by his peaceful attitude, they stopped, looked over their shoulders, and slowly and warily came back, keeping, however, at a safe distance from him. They found their voices again; again the reviling cries went forth.

"Jew! Jew! Jew!"

"Good children! good children!' said Aaron, in a clear, mellifluous voice. Then he put his pipe to his mouth again, and continued to smoke, smiling and nodding his head as if in approval.

"Jew! Jew! Jew!"

"Good little boys and girls," said Aaron. "Bravo! bravo! You deserve a reward. Every labourer is worthy of his hire."

He drew from his pocket three or four pennies, which, with smiling nods of his head, he threw among them.

Instantly came into play other passions—greed, avarice, the determination not to be defrauded of their due. Falling upon the money, they scrambled and fought for it. Aaron threw among them two or three more pennies, and their ardour increased. They scratched, they kicked, they tumbled over each other; blows were given and returned. Those who had secured pennies scampered away with them, and, with loud and vengeful cries, the penniless scampered after them. In a very little while they had all disappeared. To the victors the spoils, it

is said; but in this instance it really appeared as
if victory had ranged itself on Aaron's side.

Shaking with internal laughter, he remained on
his steps awhile, puffing at his pipe; then he put
up the shutters, locked the street door, put out the
shop lights, and rejoined his wife.

"My dear," he said, and his voice was so gay
that her heart beat with joy, "that is the end of the
first act.   They will not come back to-night."

CHAPTER XV.

THE BATTLE IS FOUGHT AND WON.

"THE personal affections by which we are governed," said Aaron Cohen, seating himself comfortably in his chair, "are, like all orders of beings to which they come, of various degrees and qualities, and the smaller become merged and lost in the larger, as the serpents of Pharaoh's magicians were swallowed up by Aaron's rod. Wisdom is better than an inheritance, and anger resteth in the bosom of fools. Moreover, as is observed by Rabbi Chanina, 'Wise men promote peace in the world.' Such, my dear Rachel, is my aim, and so long as the means within my reach are harmless, so long will I follow the learned rabbi's precept. If the human heart were not full of envy and deceit, what I have done should bring joy to our persecutors ; but I will not pledge myself that it has done so in this instance. On the contrary, on the contrary. They have something else to think of than calling me what I am proud to be called—a Jew. How they scratched and fought and ran!" Aaron paused here to laugh. "The opprobrious cries ceased suddenly, did they not, Rachel?"

"They did, and I was very much surprised."

"You will be more surprised when you hear that I rewarded with modern shekels the labours of the young rascals who would make our lives a torment to us."

"You gave them money!" exclaimed Rachel, in amazement. "Is it possible you rewarded them for their bad work?"

"I threw among them seven penny pieces. Yes, yes, I rewarded them. Why not?"

"But why?"

"Ah, why, why? Had I thrown among them seven cannon balls they would scarcely have been more effective. The truth of this will be made manifest to our benefit before many days are gone, or Cohen is not my name. Wife of my soul, I went forth, not with a lion's, but with a fox's skin. Have I not studied the law? Are not the Cohanim priests, and are not priests supposed to be men of intelligence and resource? We read in Proverbs, 'Counsel is mine, and sound wisdom; I have understanding, I have strength.' Rabbi Meyer says that the study of the law endows a man with sovereignty, dominion, and ratiocination.   He is slow to anger, ready to forgive an injury, has a good heart, receives chastisement with resignation, loves virtue, correction, and admonition.   This, perhaps, is going a little too far, and is endowing a human being with qualities too transcendent ; but it is true to a certain extent, and I have profited by the learned rabbi's words. Ill fitted should I be to engage in the battle of life if I were not able to cope with the young rascals who made the night hideous outside our door, and who, if I am not mistaken, will repeat their performance to-morrow evening at the same hour."

"They will come again !" cried Rachel, clasping her hands in despair.

"They will come again, and again, and yet again, and then—well, then we shall see what we shall see."

"You gave them money to-night," said Rachel, sadly, "and they will return for more."

"And they will return for more," said Aaron, with complacency.   "At the present moment I should judge that they are engaged in a fierce contest. When that look comes into your face, my dear, it is an indication that I have said something you do

not exactly understand. I threw to them seven
apples of discord, which the nimblest and the
strongest seized and fled with. But each soldier
conceived he had a right to at least one of the
apples, and those who were left empty-handed
laboured under a sense of wrong. They had been
robbed by their comrades. After them they rushed
to obtain their portion of the spoils of war. Then
ensued a grand scrimmage in which noses have
been injured and eyes discoloured. Even as we
converse the battle is continued. I am not there,
but I see the scene clearly with my mind's eye."
He took a sovereign from his pocket, and regarded
it contemplatively. " Ah, thou root of much evil
and of much good, what have you not to answer
for ? What blessings is it not in your power to
bestow, what evil passions do you not bring into
play ? Rachel, my love, take heart of courage, and
when you hear those boys shouting outside to-
morrow night do not be alarmed. Trust in me ;
everything will come right in the end."

The scene which Aaron had drawn from his
imagination was as near as possible to the truth.
There had been a battle royal between the boys
and girls for possession of the pennies ; noses were

put out of joint, black eyes were given, words of injurious import exchanged, and much bad blood engendered. The sevenpence for which they fought would have gone but a little way to pay for the repairs to the clothes which were torn and rent during the fray. The end of it was that the robbers, after being kicked and cuffed ignominiously, were not allowed to join in a compact made by the penniless, to the effect that they would assemble outside Aaron Cohen's shop to-morrow night and repeat the tactics which had been so well rewarded, and that all moneys received should be equally divided between the warriors engaged. One Ted Kite was appointed commander, to organise the expedition and to see fair play.

Accordingly, on Tuesday night a score or so of boys and girls presented themselves in front of the shop, and commenced shouting, "Jew! Jew! Jew!" the fugleman being Ted Kite, who proved himself well fitted for the task.

"There he is, there he is!" said the youngsters eagerly, as Aaron made his appearance on the doorstep; and, inspired by their captain, they continued to fire.

"Good children, good children," said Aaron, with

good-humoured smiles, and continuing to smoke his
silver-mounted pipe. "Very well done, very well
done indeed!"

"Ain't he going to throw us nothink?" they
asked each other anxiously, their greedy eyes
watching Aaron's movements. They were kept
rather long in suspense, but at length Aaron's hand
sought his pocket, and half a dozen pennies rattled
on the stones. Despite their compact down they
pounced, and fought and scratched for them as on
the previous night, the fortunate ones scudding
away as on the first occasion, followed by their
angry comrades. They were caught, and compelled
to disgorge; the pennies were changed into farthings,
and each soldier received one for his pay; the two
or three that were left were spent in sweetstuff.

"What a game!" the children exclaimed, and
appointed to meet on the following night to continue the pastime.

On this third night they were kept waiting still
longer. Aaron Cohen did not make his appearance
so quickly, and several minutes elapsed before the
pennies were thrown to them. On the first night
he had disbursed seven, on the second night six,
on this third only four. There was the usual

fighting for them, and the usual scampering away; but when the sum-total was placed in the hands of Ted Kite a great deal of dissatisfaction was expressed. Only fourpence! They doubted the correctness of the sum; they were sure that more had been thrown; one girl said she counted eight, and others supported her statement. Who had stolen the missing pennies? They quarrelled and fought again; they regarded each other with suspicion; doubts were thrown upon the honesty of the captain. Off went his coat instantly; off went the coats of other boys; the girls, having no coats to throw off, tucked up their sleeves; and presently six or seven couples were hitting, scratching, and kicking each other. Much personal damage was done, and more bad blood engendered. The warfare was not by any means of a heroic nature.

Nevertheless they assembled on the fourth night, and were kept waiting still longer before they were paid. Aaron did not show his liberality, however, until he had had a conference with the captain. His keen eyes had singled out Ted Kite, and he beckoned to him. Ted hesitated; he was only a small boy; Aaron Cohen was a big man, and in a personal contest could have disposed of him comfortably.

"Yah, yer coward!" cried the rank and file to their captain. "What are yer frightened at? What did we make yer captain for?"

Thus taunted, Ted Kite ventured to approach the smiling foe.

"Come a little nearer," said Aaron; "I am not going to hurt you. I wish you to do me a favour."

Ted, with a sidelong look over his shoulders at his army, as if appealing to it to rush to his rescue in case he was seized, shuffled forward. Aaron Cohen held out his hand; Ted Kite timidly responded, and was surprised at the friendly grip he received.

"You are the leader," said Aaron, in his most genial voice.

"Yes, Mr. Cohen," replied Ted, growing bold, "I'm the captain."

"Clever lad, clever captain! Here's a penny for you. Don't let them see you take it. It is for you alone. They will do as you tell them, of course."

"I'll let 'em know it if they don't."

"It's right you should. I think it is very kind of you to come here as you do, but I want you to oblige me and not come to-morrow night. It is Friday, and the shop will be closed; so you would be wasting your time. That would be foolish, would it not ? "

" Yes, it would," said Ted, somewhat bewildered. " Shall we come on Saturday night? "

" Certainly, if you think proper. Then you will not be here to-morrow ? "

" We won't, as you'd rather not, Mr. Cohen."

" Thank you, I am really obliged to you. Now go and join your army."

Ted Kite turned away, walked a step or two, and returned.

" But I say, Mr. Cohen―― "

" Well, my lad ? "

" Do you like it ? "

" Do I like it ? " echoed Aaron, with a sly chuckle. " Should I speak to you as I am doing if I didn't ? I think it is very nice of you ; very nice, very nice indeed ! "

" Oh ! " said Ted, in a crest-fallen tone. As Aaron took pleasure in the persecution, it was not half such good fun as it had been. " He says he likes it," he said to his comrades, when he was among them.

" How much did he give yer? " they inquired,

feeling as he did in respect of the fun of their proceedings.

" He didn't give me nothink."

" We sor him hold out his hand to yer," they protested.

"You sor us shake hands, that's what yer saw. Let's get on with the game ; we don't want to be kept waiting here all night."

They went on with the game, calling "Jew! Jew! Jew!" half-heartedly. Putting the pecuniary reward out of the question, it was a game that was becoming rather monotonous. They had to call for quite a quarter of an hour before Aaron paid them ; and this time he paid them with two pennies only. The children fell on the ground, and scraped the stones for more, but found none ; and they retired grumbling, discontented, and suspicious of each other's honesty.

On Friday night, the Sabbath eve, Aaron and Rachel had peace ; and on Saturday night the children made their appearance again and gave forth their chorus. Aaron came to the door, and stood there, smoking his pipe, and smiling at them ; but he did not throw any pennies to them. They did not know what to make of it. Their voices grew weaker and weaker, they wandered about discontentedly, they declared it was not fair on Mr. Cohen's part. "We'll try him agin on Monday night," they said.

They tried him again on Monday night, and he stood on his steps, commending them, but he gave them no more pennies. There was no heart whatever now in their invectives. They were not philosophers, and did not know that the course Aaron had pursued had taken the sting out of their tails. "He likes it," they said to one another, as they strolled off moodily, "and he wants us to come here and scream our throats dry without being paid for it. Well, we ain't going to do it. We won't call him Jew any more, if he wants us ever so much. It ain't likely, now, is it? What does he mean by treating us so shabby?" These young rapscallions thought the world was out of joint.

On this Monday night an incident occurred which never came to Aaron's ears. Prissy, hearing of the annoyance to which the Cohens were subjected, made her appearance as the boys were wandering disconsolately away, and without wasting time in asking questions, darted like a tiger-cat upon the biggest of them, and fixed her fingers in his hair.

She had left Victoria Regina asleep on the coals
in her aunt's shop, and had, so to speak, girded up
her loins for the contest, by pinning up her ragged
skirts and tucking up her sleeves to the shoulder.
" What's that for?" cried the boy, struggling to
get free. Prissy vouchsafed no explanation; the
only words she uttered were addressed to the other
boys. " Fair play. One at a time. I'm only a
gal." Chivalry was not dead. They stood round
the combatants, and witnessed the fight without
interfering. It was a desperate encounter. Many
an ugly blow did Prissy receive ; but she depended
upon her talons, and pulled such quantities of hair
out of the big boy's head, and scratched his face so
dreadfully, that he was at length driven to tears and
entreaties to her to leave off. " Do yer want any
more?" screamed Prissy, whose breath was almost
gone. The big boy's answer was to run away,
whimpering, and the other boys hooted him as he
fled. " Would any other boy like to come on?"
demanded the panting Prissy. Not one accepted
the challenge, and Prissy, glaring at them as they
followed their vanquished comrade, went back to
Victoria Regina, and shed copious tears of indignant
satisfaction over the sleeping babe.

In this way it was that Aaron Cohen fought the battle and gained a bloodless victory. He laughed in his sleeve as he thought of it, and laughed aloud in his cosy little parlour when he related the whole affair to Rachel.

"One shilling and eightpence has it cost me, my love," he said, "and I do not grudge the money. Show me the battle that has been won for less."

Rachel was greatly relieved; but her dominant feeling was admiration for her husband's wisdom.

"I do not believe any other man in the world would have thought of it," she said; and though Aaron shook his head in modest deprecation, he was justified in inwardly congratulating himself upon his astute tactics.

The story got about, and the townspeople were much amused by it. "Mr. Cohen's a clever fellow," they said. He grew to be respected by them, and as the weeks passed by and it was seen that he was not only a fair-dealing but a kindly-hearted man, the innuendoes which Mr. Whimpole continued to circulate about him produced a very small effect. Mr. Whimpole was not pleased; where is the man who would have been in his position? Talking one night

with Rachel over the animosity the corn-chandler
bore towards the Jews, Aaron said,—

"I have no doubt, my dear, that he is quite conscientious, and that he considers his prejudices to be
the outcome of a just conviction. Doubtless his
parents had the same conviction, and he imbibed it
from them. There are thousands of people who
agree with him, and there are worse persecutions than
that to which we have been subjected. Look at that
infamously-governed country, Russia, which, in the
maps, ought to be stamped blood-red, with a heavy
mourning border around it! The wretches who
inflict incredible sufferings upon countless innocent
beings call themselves Christians. They are not
Christians, they are fiends, and a judgment will fall
upon them. Spain, once the greatest of nations, fell
into decay when the Jews deserted it. So will it be
with other nations that oppress the Jew. Let
Germany look to it. It is easy to arouse the evil
passions of human beings, but a brand of fire shall
fall upon the heads of those who are employed in
work so vile."

CHAPTER XVI.

PERHAPS, however, to Rachel may chiefly be ascribed the general esteem in which the Cohens were held by the townsfolk. Charitable, kind, and gentle by nature, she was instinctively drawn to all poor people who had fallen into misfortune. Here there was no question of Jew and Christian. A human being was in trouble; that was sufficient for this dear woman, whose heart bled at the sight of suffering. Upon her sympathetic ears no tale of distress could fall without bearing fruit. Now it was a basin of nourishing soup, now a mould of jelly, now part of a chicken, cooked by herself, and paid for out of her housekeeping money. She won friends everywhere, and her sweet face was like a ray of sunshine in the homes of the poor. It was not at all uncommon to hear that her timely assistance had been the means of restoring to health those who had been stricken down. She walked through life as an angel of mercy

might have done, and spiritual flowers grew about
her feet.

Of all the friends who sounded her praises none
were more enthusiastic than little Prissy, who
came now regularly to the house to do domestic
work.

Anxious to increase his trade, Aaron had stocked
his shop with such articles of wear and adornment
which were most in request. He had not the means
to pay ready money for the stock, but through a
friend in Portsmouth, Mr. Moss, with whom the
readers of this story have already become acquainted,
he obtained credit from wholesale dealers who would
have been chary to trust him without a sufficient
recommendation. Apart from the pleasures which
his modest success in business afforded him, there
was a happiness in store for him to which he looked
forward with a sense of profound gratitude. Rachel
was about to become a mother. To this fond couple,
who lived only for each other, there could be no
greater joy than this. They had lost their firstborn,
and God was sending another child to bless their
days. They never closed their eyes at night, they
never rose in the morning, without offering a prayer
of thanks to the Most High for His goodness to

them. They saw no cloud gathering to darken their happiness.

It was an ordinary event, for which Aaron could hardly have been prepared.

They had been eleven months in Gosport when one morning Aaron, rising first and going down to his shop, found that burglars had been at work. They had effected an entrance at the back of the house, and had carried away the most valuable articles in the window. The loss, Aaron calculated, would not be less than a hundred pounds.

It was, to him, a serious loss ; he had commenced with a very small capital, and his earnings during the year had left only a small margin over his household and trade expenses. His business was growing, it is true, but for the first six months he had barely paid his way ; it was to the future he looked to firmly establish himself, and now in one night all his profits were swept away. More than this ; if he were called upon to pay his debts he would have but a few pounds left. Rachel, whose health the last week or two had been delicate, her confinement being so near, was in bed by his directions ; he had forbidden her to rise till ten o'clock. It was a matter to be thankful for ; he could keep the shock of the loss from her ; in her condition bad news might have a serious effect upon her.

He set everything in order, spoke no word of what had occurred to his wife, re-arranged the shop window, and took down the shutters. In the course of the day he told Rachel that he intended to close a couple of hours earlier than usual ; he had to go to Portsmouth upon business in the evening, and should be absent probably till near midnight.

"You will not mind being alone, my love?" he . said.

"Oh no," she answered, with a tender smile ; "I have plenty to occupy me."

She had been for some time busy with her needle preparing for her unborn child.

"But you must go to bed at ten," said Aaron. "I shall lock the shop, and take the key of the back door with me, so that I can let myself in."

She promised to do as he bade her, and in the evening he left her to transact his business. He had no fear that she would be intruded upon ; it was not likely that the house would be broken into two nights in succession ; besides, with the exception of some pledges of small value which he kept in the safe, where they were secure from burglars, there was little now to tempt thieves to repeat their knavish doings. So with fond kisses he bade her good-night.

They stood facing each other, looking into each other's eyes. Rachel's eyes were of a tender grey, with a light so sweet in them that he never looked into them unmoved. He kissed them now with a strange yearning at his heart.

"I hope baby's eyes will be like yours, dear love," he said; "the soul of sweetness and goodness shines in them."

She smiled happily, and pressed him fondly to her. Ah, if he had known!

His first business was with the police. He went to the station, and telling the inspector of his loss, said that he wished it to be kept private, because of his fear that it might reach his wife's ears. The inspector replied that it would be advisable under any circumstances. Leaving in the officer's hands a list of the articles that had been stolen, he proceeded to Portsmouth to consult his friend Mr. Moss. That good-hearted gentleman was deeply concerned at the news.

" It is a serious thing, Cohen," he said.

" A very serious thing," replied Aaron, gravely ; " but I shall overcome it. Only I require time. I promised to pay some bills to-morrow, and as I shall need a little stock to replace what I have lost, it will cramp me to do so now."

He mentioned the names of the tradesmen to whom he had given the promise, and asked Mr. Moss to call upon them in the morning and explain the matter to them.

" They will not lose their money," he said ; " it will |not take me very long to make everything right."

" I will see them," said Mr. Moss, " and I am sure they will give you time. Aaron Cohen's name is a sufficient guarantee."

" I hope it will always be," replied Aaron. " It is very unfortunate just now, because I have extra expenses coming on me. The nurse, the doctor—— "

" I know, I know. How is Mrs. Cohen ? "

" Fairly well, I am glad to say. She knows nothing of what has occurred."

" Of course not. How could you tell her while she is like that ? When Mrs. Moss is in the same way I am always singing and laughing and saying cheerful things to her. Between you and me, we expect an addition ourselves in about four months."

" Indeed! That will make—— "

" Twelve," said Mr. Moss, rubbing his hands briskly together. " Increase and multiply. It's our bounden duty ; eh, Cohen ? "

"Yes," said Aaron, rather absently. " And now I must go ; it will be late before I reach home, and for all Rachel's promises I expect she will keep awake for me. Good-night, and thank you."

" Nothing to thank me for. Good-night, and good luck."

When Aaron returned to Gosport it was midnight. Winter was coming on, and it was cold and dark. Buttoning his coat close up to his neck, he hastened his steps.

He was not despondent. Misfortune had fallen upon him, but he had confidence in himself ; and, despite the practical common sense which showed itself in all his actions, there was in his nature an underlying current of spiritual belief in Divine assistance towards the successful accomplishment of just and worthy endeavour. That it is man's duty to do right, to work, to pray, to be considerate to his neighbours, to make his home cheerful, to be as charitable as his means will allow—this was his creed; and it was strengthened by his conviction that God made Himself manifest even upon earth in matters of right and wrong. He did not relegate the expiation of transgression to the future; he did not believe that a man could wipe out the sins of the past year by fasting, and praying, and beating his breast on the Day of Atonement. Wrong-doing was not to be set aside and forgotten until a convenient hour for repentance arrived. That was the conduct of a man who tried to cheat his conscience, who deluded himself with the hope that the Eternal sometimes slept. Daily, hourly, a man must keep watch over himself and his actions. This had been his rule of life; and it contributed to his happiness, and to the happiness of those around him.

He was within a quarter of a mile of his residence when he was conscious of an unseen disturbance in the air; and presently he saw a distant glare in the sky, and the faint echoes of loud voices stole upon his senses. Agitated as he had been by what had transpired during this long unfortunate day, he could not at first be certain whether these signs were real or imaginary; but he soon discovered that they did not spring from his imagination. The glare in the sky became plainly visible, the loud voices reached his ears. There was a fire in the town, and he was proceeding towards it. Instantly his thoughts, his fears, centred upon Rachel. He ran forward quickly, and found himself struggling through an excited crowd. Flames shot upwards; the air was filled with floating sparks of fire. Great God! It was his own house that was being destroyed by the devouring element. He did not heed that; the destruction of his worldly goods did not affect him.

"My wife!" he screamed. "Where is my wife?"

By main force they held him back, for he was rushing into the flames.

"Let me go!" he screamed. "Where is my wife?"

"It is all right, Mr. Cohen," a number of voices replied. "She is saved!"

"Thank God, oh, thank God!" he cried. "Take me to her. Where is she?"

He cared not for the ruin that had overtaken him; like cool water to a parched throat had come the joyful news.

" Take me to her. In the name of Heaven, tell me where she is ! "

She was in a house, at a safe distance from the fire, and thither he was led. Rachel was lying on a couch in her nightdress ; sympathising people were about her.

" Rachel, Rachel ! " he cried, and fell upon his knees by her side.

She did not answer him ; she was insensible.

" Do not agitate yourself," said a voice. It was that of a physician who had been attending to her. " Be thankful that she lives."

" O Lord, I thank Thee ! " murmured the stricken man. " My Rachel lives ! "

What mattered all the rest ? What mattered worldly ruin and destruction ? The beloved of his heart was spared to him.

" You are a sensible man, Mr. Cohen," said the physician, " and you must be calm for her sake. In her condition there will be danger if she witnesses your agitation when she recovers."

" I will be calm, sir," said Aaron, humbly. " She is all I have in the world."

He made no inquiries as to the cause of the fire ; he did not stir from Rachel's side, but sat with his eyes fixed upon her pallid face. The physician remained with them an hour, and then took his departure, saying he would return early in the morning, and leaving instructions to Aaron what to do.

At sunrise Rachel awoke. Passing one hand over her eyes, she held out the other in a groping, uncertain way. Aaron took it in his, and held it fondly; the pallor left her cheeks.

" It is you, my dear ? " she murmured.

"Yes, it is I, my life !" he said, in a low and gentle tone.

" You are well—you are safe ? "

" I am well ; I am safe," he replied. " And you, Rachel, how do you feel ? "

" I have a slight headache. It will soon pass away. Oh, my dear husband, how thankful I am ! When did you return ? "

" Not till you were taken from the house. Do not talk now. Rest, rest, my beloved ! "

The endearing words brought a glad smile to her lips.

" I will sleep presently, Aaron. Is the doctor here ? "

" No, but he will come soon. Shall I go for him ? "

" I can wait, dear ; when he comes I should like to speak to him alone."

"You are hurt !" he said, alarmed. " Tell me ! "

" I am not hurt, dear ; it is only that my head aches a little. He will give me something to relieve me. Have no fear for me, Aaron ; I am in no danger ; indeed, indeed, I am not ! "

" God be praised ! "

She drew his head to her breast, and they lay in silence awhile, fondly embracing.

" Let me tell you, dear, and then I will go to sleep again. I went to bed at ten, as you bade me, and though I had it in my mind to keep awake for you I could not do so. I do not know how long I slept, but I awoke in confusion, and there was a strong glare in my eyes. I hardly remember what followed. I heard voices calling to me—Prissy's voice was the loudest, I think—and then I felt that strong arms were around me, and I was being carried from the house. That is all, my dear, till I heard your voice, here. Where am I ? "

He informed her ; and then, holding him close to her, she fell asleep again. As the clock struck nine the physician entered the room, and Aaron told him what had passed.

"I can spare half an hour," said the physician. "Go and see after your affairs. I will not leave her till you return."

Kissing Rachel tenderly, and smoothing the hair from her forehead, Aaron left the house, and went to his own. Before he departed he learned from the kind neighbours, who had given Rachel shelter, that they were not in a position to keep her and Aaron with them, and he said that he would make arrangements to remove her in the course of the day, if the doctor thought it would be safe to do so. His own house, he found, was completely destroyed, but he heard of another at no great distance, which was to be let furnished for a few weeks; and this he took at once, and installed Prissy therein, to light fires and get the rooms warm. The arrangement completed, he hastened back to Rachel, between whom and the physician a long consultation had taken place during his absence. At the conclusion of their conversation she had asked him one question,—

"Shall I be so all my life, doctor?"

"I fear so," was his reply.

"My poor husband!" she murmured. "My poor, dear husband! Say nothing to him, doctor,

I implore you. Let him hear the truth from my lips."

He consented, not sorry to be spared a painful duty. "She is surprisingly well," he said to Aaron, "and in a few days will be able to get about a little, though you must not expect her to be quite strong till her child is born."

The news was so much better than Aaron expected, that he drew a deep breath of exquisite relief.

"Can she be removed to-day with safety?" he asked.

"I think so. She will be happier with you alone. Give me your new address; I will call and see her there this evening."

At noon she was taken in a cab to her new abode, and Aaron carried her in, and laid her on the sofa before a bright fire. In the evening the physician called according to his promise. "She is progressing famously," he said to Aaron. "Get her to bed early, and it may be advisable that she should keep there a few days. But I shall speak more definitely about this later on. Mr. Cohen, you have my best wishes. You are blessed with a noble wife." Tears shone in Aaron's eyes. "Let me impress upon you," continued the doctor, "to be strong as she is

strong ; but at present, with the birth of her child
so near, it is scarcely physical power that sustains
her. She is supported by a spiritual strength drawn
from her love for you and her unborn babe."

With these words the physician left them together.
Prissy was gone, and Aaron and Rachel were
alone.

They exchanged but few words. Rachel still
occupied the couch before the fire, and as she seemed
to be dozing Aaron would not disturb her. Thus
an hour passed by, and then Rachel said,—

" The doctor advises me to go to bed early. Will
you help me up, dear ? "

She stood on her feet before him, and as his eyes
rested on her face a strange fear entered his heart.

"Come, my life !" he said.

" A moment, dear husband," she said. " I have
something to tell you, something that will grieve
you. I do not know how it happened, nor does the
good doctor know. He has heard of only one such
case before. I am not in pain ; I do not suffer. It
is much to be grateful for, and I am humbly, humbly
grateful. It might have been so much worse !"

" Rachel, my beloved !" said Aaron, placing his
hands on her shoulders.

"Keep your arms about me, my honoured husband. Let me feel your dear hands, your dear face. Kiss me, Aaron. May I tell you now?"

"Tell me now, my beloved."

"Look into my eyes, dear. I cannot look into yours. Dear husband, I am blind!"

END OF VOL. I.

Printed by Hazell, Watson, & Viney, Ld., London and Aylesbury.

www.ingramcontent.com/pod-product-compliance
Lightning Source LLC
Chambersburg PA
CBHW020606030726
47497CB00007B/2098